HER DRAGON KING

BIANCA COLE

CONTENTS

Dragons and witches never mix, but she is mine.

My father's sudden death means I have to select a wife.

A ball is set up with an invitation to all the dragon princesses.

I'm told I have to select a bride by the end of the night, but I'm not feeling it.

Until she steps into the room.

A woman who most certainly isn't royalty.

My dragon roars to attention, recognizing her as my mate.

I ask her to dance to the disgust of everyone else.

I don't care what they think.

I don't care that my mate is a witch.

I don't care that this will cause an uproar when the truth is revealed.

She needs my help to locate her family, and I can't deny her anything.

I want to claim her and make her mine, but I have to win her trust.

Dark secrets behind her family's capture will test our bond.

I'm determined to overcome the odds and claim her —no matter what.

AIDEN

"I'm sorry sire, but I must insist," Lance, my royal aid says.

"Fuck's sake, Lance," I growl, slamming my hand down on the desk. "I'm too fucking young for this shit."

He bows his head at the tone in my voice. "Sir, I understand it is not ideal, but——"

"But, nothing." I crack my neck, feeling rage pulse through my veins. If he's not careful, I will turn and burn him to a crisp. He has no fucking empathy at all. "My father died three days ago, and you are already setting up a ball for me to find a wife. We just got back from his funeral, damn it."

He pales as my dragon beings to rear his head— anger. It's all I've felt since my father's murder three days ago. I don't want to take a wife. I want to track down the bastard that killed him.

Lance is an inconsiderate asshole. He is also right.

The dragon shifter outcasts, who murdered my father, will want to target me next. If I can find a wife who will provide me with an heir, our family's position will remain secure. It's crucial that the royal lineage continues. He insists I take a wife tomorrow evening.

I'm thirty years old, and for a dragon, it is young. To be forced to take a wife so early sucks, especially as she won't be my mate.

"I do apologize for the timing, but there are rumors of an uprising in the north."

"There have been rumors of an uprising in the fucking north since before I was born, Lance." I shake my head. "What makes this time any different to before?"

He eyes me cautiously. "This time, they succeeded in killing your father."

My jaw clenches and I spin around, walking toward the dresser in the corner. I grab a bottle of bourbon and pour myself a glass. If Lance knows what's best for him, he will leave. He's grating on my last nerve, and my dragon wants out. I chuck back the smoky whiskey, letting it burn on the way down.

"Sir, do I have your approval to hold the ball?" Lance asks.

I tighten my grip on the whiskey glass, slamming it down.

The fear in the air increases, and my dragon enjoys it. He's ready to break free. Instead of answering my aid, I march toward the patio door of my bedroom and walk onto the large balcony.

I throw my jacket down on the floor, before unbuttoning my shirt and leaving it on top.

"What are you doing, Aiden?" Lance asks.

I still don't acknowledge him. It's pretty fucking obvious what I'm doing. Maybe I need to sack Lance. It's been all of seventy-two hours since I became king, and he is pissing me off.

I unbutton my pants and leave them there, before letting go. Red scales prickle over every inch of my body as I begin to shift.

"Is this the time to shift?" he asks.

I roar at him, my dragon taking over entirely. He wants to burn my royal aid to a crisp, but I won't let him. Instead, I launch off the balcony, enjoying the free fall for a moment, before flapping my vast wings and rising into the air.

I don't look back, letting myself break free. My father's death has filled me with a pain I can't process yet. He has always been here. The stability I've relied on all my life. I'm too young to be king. All my family is gone, either dead or left here.

I fly out of the valley in between the mountains where my castle is situated, rising higher and higher. This is what I need right now, not a ball to find a fucking wife. I need to be free. A chance to clear my head. It hasn't even been two hours since we buried my father, and he wants a ball tomorrow evening.

I can hear my father lecturing me in my head.

Aiden, you have responsibilities to our people.

He wouldn't approve of the way I'm acting, but I can't help it. I've never handled grief well. I've also never handled my position and destiny well either.

Lake Tahoe glistens like crystals as the hot sun beats down on its surface. I soar down, flapping my wings to glide across the water, dipping my talons in as I go. The fish dart away beneath the surface as I move over their home. This is my favorite thing to do, shift, and escape everything over the lake and mountains.

It's indescribable the way it makes me feel. A freedom that I only get when I allow the beast to take over. Dragon shifters don't shift enough nowadays. So many are trying to be more human and suppress their dragon half, which makes no sense to me.

Dragons have a terrible reputation because of a few who were unable to control themselves when we were first revealed. We always lived in the mountains, hiding from humans beforehand. The few that couldn't control themselves burned cities or towns to the ground, wreaking havoc. In turn, it gave our entire kind a bad name. Humans are scared of us, but they fraternize with the wolf shifters.

Witches and warlocks may be fighting against us, but wolf shifters are our natural enemy and have been for millennia. I twist around and fly back over the lake, before soaring into the sky.

I fly toward a mountain peak and search it to ensure

it's clear, before unleashing my fire. It melts the snow-capped peaks but gives me a release of energy. Suddenly, a black dragon flies over the other side, shocking me.

Charles.

I fly to the mountain peak and land, and so does he. He has been my best friend since I can remember. I shift back into my human form on the recently melted peak.

"What are you doing here?" I ask, smiling.

He shrugs. "I saw you take off back at the castle, and I wanted to have some fun too."

I slump down on a rock. "I can't believe he is dead."

Charles walks over to me and sets a hand on my shoulder before sitting down too. We've been friends so long neither of us cares about our state of undress. It's natural for dragon shifters to be comfortable naked, but we adopt clothes to keep humans at ease. "I know it was a shock." A small silence passes between us. "Have they got any closer to finding out who did it?"

I shake my head. "No, not yet."

He sighs. "I'm so sorry, Aiden. What got you wound up enough to shift?"

"Lance."

He shakes his head. "That man is an asshole."

I laugh. "You could say that again. He insists on throwing a ball tomorrow night." I shake my head. "We buried him today, and he wants me to pick a princess to marry tomorrow."

Charles claps me on the back. "A princess, hey?

Well, that can't be too bad. A perfect distraction from everything else."

I look my best friend in the eye. "You can't mean that. Dragons aren't built to take a life partner that isn't their mate."

A sadness ignites in his eyes. "That's true, but it's becoming increasingly rare for us to find our mates. The world is changing, Aiden, and I'm not sure it's for the better." His brow furrows. "I mean, the king of the fae has taken a human mate. That's insane considering how stuck up the fae are." He shakes his head. "Hundreds of years ago no dragons, wolves or fae mated to their kind, always."

I nod. "You are saying we may be fated to be with a mate outside of our species." The fae king has recently been reaching out to my father, who wouldn't indulge him. He wants to put together a council and unite all of our species. It's ambitious. I wonder if he will approach me now my father is dead.

He smiles wistfully. "Unfortunately, yes."

I glance down across the lake. "Is that such a bad thing?"

Charles claps me on the back. "Who knows? I, used to think we all need to integrate instead of segregating, but since the truth came out, this world seems worse, not better."

I draw in a deep breath. "I think you are right." I run a hand through my hair. "I'm just not ready to pick some random princess to marry."

He nods. "Then don't. Indulge Lance and allow him to throw the ball, just don't pick one of the princesses." He shrugs. "Unless she is your mate, of course."

I roll my eyes. "The chances of that are about zero, but I guess you're right."

He smiles. "I'm always right."

"Don't be a cocky asshole." I shove him in the shoulder. "I guess I better get back." I stare in the direction of my home, wanting nothing more than to shift and fly the other way, never looking back. It would be a whole lot easier than facing reality.

"I know that look. What's up?" Charles asks.

I shake my head. "Nothing."

He raises a brow. "We've known each other since we were kids, you know you can't lie to me."

I sigh heavily. "It feels like everyone I love I'm destined to lose. I've got no family anymore."

Charles claps me on the back. "That's not true, what about Elaine?"

I glare at him. "What about her? She abandoned me and left me with our father."

He nods. "Yes, she did, but don't tell me you wouldn't have done the same if you met your mate."

He has a point—every dragon pines for their mate. If I found out mine had been a wolf shifter, I would have left too. My father wouldn't have been happy, but I'm sure I wouldn't let him stand in the way or my happiness.

"True. Would you?" I ask, meeting the gaze of my childhood friend.

There's a flash of something in his eyes. "I don't know. It wouldn't be such a big deal for me. I'm not a prince." He turns tense and nods his head toward the mountain across the lake. "Race you back?"

I smile. "You're on."

We both shift at the same time and soar into the sky. At least I've still got Charles. He's the closest thing left to family, except Elaine. I don't hold out any hope for salvaging our relationship.

I saw her at the funeral, but I'm too ashamed to face her. When father wanted to break her bond with that wolf, I did nothing. I stood by and watched as he drove her out of our lives.

I fly over the mountain, pushing faster than Charles. I let the wind against my wings and the rush of air past my ears drown out all my worries for the moment. Right now, I'm free from them. I'll just have to face them tomorrow.

2

ILSA

*M*y heart pounds frantically in my chest as I drive into the parking lot of the grand castle. This is dangerous. I'm not an idiot, crashing a dragon shifter party as a witch is a big deal. We're not exactly on friendly terms with the shifters.

I've run out of options, and every clue leads to the deceased king. Since I can't ask him where my family is, his son seems like the next best option. King Aiden is due to select a wife tonight at a royal ball, if the rumors I've heard are true.

The ball is my only chance to get anywhere near him, but I'm going to have to be careful. If they realize I'm an uninvited witch, they will see me as a threat. Some of the witches joined with the dragon shifters, and I'm sure many will be in attendance.

I don't know if they will have a guest list. Magic is the only thing that will get me in. It's risky, though. If anyone detects my use of magic, I'll end up dead. I park my beat-up old mustang far away and step out of the car, making sure to smooth down my dress.

The cars in the parking lot are all new and sparkly, and mine is a rust bucket. It stands out like a sore thumb. I can only hope that I don't stand out as well. I picked the best dress I own to wear, but from the look of some of the people walking into the castle, it's not nearly good enough.

Before I make it near enough to the main entrance for people to spot me, I slip into a walled garden to one side and quickly change my dress with magic. It will help me get in, but I'm not sure how long the spell will last until it switches back.

I glance down at the intricate gold and white lace adorning my body, wishing I had the money to afford a dress like this.

I slip back out of the garden and walk casually toward the entrance. My heart hammers against my rib cage as my heels click on the tarmac. There is a short line of people waiting at the door, holding their invites. I didn't even consider that this party would have invitations. I assumed there would be a guest list.

Who the hell even does that anymore?

Royal dragon shifters, it seems. I breathe deeply, trying to calm my nerves. If I get in there, I'll need a stiff drink or maybe ten. Two guards stand either side of the door, one of them is holding a clipboard. He's taking the names of guests and invitations.

I rack my brain, trying to figure out my plan. It would be easy to conjure up my name on the list, but I can't replicate an invitation without seeing one.

As I get to the front, the guard's brow furrows as his eyes drag down my body. "Name?"

I sneeze, knowing it will be enough to hide my use of magic as I make sure my name is on the list. "Oh, sorry. My name is Ilsa Black, and I forgot my invitation at home. My name should be on the list," I say, trying my best to give him a confident stare.

His eyes narrow as they move to the clipboard. He scans it and starts to shake his head before stopping. "Oh, yes, I've found it." He nods his head toward the door. "Go on in."

I smile and slip past him into the castle. My heart is hammering as I move away from the guards. "Wait," he shouts after me.

I freeze, slowly turning around to glance at him.

My heart is frozen until I see him holding my purse. "I think you dropped this."

I roll my eyes and walk back to him. "Of course, I'm such a klutz." I take the purse. "Thank you."

He says nothing as I spin around and head into the castle. I seriously thought he'd caught onto me then. Dragon shifters are good at sensing magic intervention. Luckily for me, the shifters on the door aren't the brightest bunch.

I've only just got in here, and my nerves are wrecked. The sign for the bathroom catches my attention, and I slip that way. If I'm going to pull this off, I need to make sure I'm on top form. Thankfully, there is no one inside, so I walk to the sink and run the taps.

I stare at myself in the mirror, wondering what the hell I'm doing here. This isn't me. I've never been the hero that swoops in to save the day. That has always been my brother. The problem is, he's one of the people I'm here to find.

If the king knows where my family is, I need to question him—no matter the risks. I splash some water on my face and over my neck, trying to cool myself down. My heart is pounding too fast. At this rate, I'll never get the courage to approach the king. I've bitten off more than I can chew.

The door swings open behind me, making me jump. A woman walks in, hardly glancing at me, but I recognize her. Alena, she's a witch—one of the ones who was excluded from the coven when she decided to side with the dragons.

Dragons and witches have been at war for years. It all started when the new king's grandfather double-crossed the leader of the coven. She couldn't let it go and decided to declare war, but they are too strong for witches. They have a certain resistance to magic when shifted.

I keep my face forward, hoping she won't notice me.

"Ilsa, I'm surprised to see you here," she says, walking to stand by my side. "Are you considering joining the dragons?" She raises a brow.

I nod, unable to trust myself to speak.

"Who invited you?" she asks.

Oh shit. I don't know any dragons. The only dragon's name I know is the kings. "Aiden."

Her eyes widen, and then she laughs. "Surely not, the king wouldn't invite a witch to the ball." She crosses her arms over her chest. "What are you doing here, Ilsa?"

This is the last thing I need. I wasn't expecting to be ambushed by a witch the moment I got into the castle. "I wanted to speak with the king, that's all." I shrug and glance back at the sink, turning the taps off.

"Ilsa, I'm not stupid. If you are here to cause trouble, I will have to report you." She moves for the door.

I grab her arm. "Please, Alena, I'm not here to cause trouble." I hate the desperation in my voice. "I am only here to ask the king one question."

She yanks her arm from me. "What question?"

I search Alena's eyes, knowing she isn't heartless. She may have picked the dragon's side in the war, but she has compassion. "My family is missing, and I wanted to find out if he knows where they are."

"Rowan and Irene are missing?" she asks.

I nod. "Yes, and my brother, Eric."

Her brow furrows. "What makes you think the king will know where they are?"

This is a risk. If I tell Alena what happened, she could use it against me. At the same time, if I keep it from her, she could get me thrown out. I need to speak to the king at any cost tonight. "It's a hunch. My brother met with the king's father the day they disappeared."

She sighs heavily. "Your parents were the best of that coven. They weren't judgmental of me." Her face looks pained as she stares into space. "Your mom even pleaded for the coven to open their mind to seeking peace with the dragons."

I take her hand. "She believes the war we are fighting is pointless. Our numbers are so low now." I squeeze gently. "There isn't a coven anymore, not really."

She squeezes my hand back. "Don't worry, Ilsa. Your parents stood up for me when no one else would. I won't turn their daughter in."

A flood of relief spirals through me. "Thank you, Alena."

"It's nothing. If you get a chance, try and find me after you speak to the king, I might be able to help you if you find something out." She narrows her eyes. "I never trusted Kendall, Aiden's father. Something may be going on that we're unaware of, but Aiden is different."

I tilt my head to the side. "In what way?"

She smiles. "You'll find out once you speak to him. He's got a kind heart, beneath all that alpha, dragon bullshit. His father didn't."

It puts me at ease a little to hear that Aiden is genuinely a nice guy. Maybe he will be happy to help me out and tell me what he knows—if he knows anything. It was his father's involvement that drew me here, not his.

"I'll try and find you later. Thank you again." I squeeze her hand and then move past her toward the door.

"Be careful, though, Ilsa. Remember, you are an enemy in their territory. Dragons don't often see reason when it comes to trespassing witches."

I swallow hard and give her a nod before heading out of the bathroom and back down the corridor. My heels click on the floor as I make it back to the entry into the ballroom. This place is so over the top.

There's a small queue of people waiting at the huge, carved oak doors in front of me. I stand in line and wait, and my stomach knots with nerves. It's time to find out the truth about my family's disappearance. All I can do is hope things go my way, but up to now, it's not been smooth sailing.

I deserve a fucking break. Ever since my parents and brother went missing, it seems like the world is trying to break me down. I won't give up, not until I'm dead.

3

AIDEN

"May I present princess Jenna," Lance says, pointing at a young, dark-haired girl who looks to be about eighteen years old—way too young to be getting married.

I give him a warning glance. He has got to be fucking kidding me. I could eat this girl for breakfast. If they force me to marry a princess that I don't love, I want one with a bit of something about her—a spark and fire. This dragon shifter couldn't stand by my side. There's no chance in hell.

"Nice to meet you," I grumble, not even bothering to bow to her.

The ball is all a waste of time. Especially if these are the women he's bringing for me. I turn away from her and head through the crowd, making a beeline for the bar. I need a fucking drink.

Tonight is a joke. The three princesses Lance has

introduced me to were all too young or too dense to hold a conversation. I push through the crowd toward the bar and lean on the counter. My rage is flaring out of control tonight, even though I was sure to have a long fly about beforehand.

My dragon is restless. I guess that's what happens when you try to force a part of you that only believes in fated mates to submit to life with a woman who isn't. I rub the space between my eyes, feeling a migraine starting. The last thing I need right now is a headache.

"What can I get you, sir?" the bartender asks me.

I don't even look up to reply. "Large bourbon, on the rocks."

"Coming right up," she says, walking away from me.

I stand up straight and run a hand across the back of my neck.

"Aiden, is that you?" I tense, hearing her voice. My sister hasn't been back here in four years, and suddenly my father dies, and she returns. I saw her at the funeral but deliberately avoided her. Not only am I ashamed for not sticking up for her, but I'm also angry that she left me with our father.

I don't even turn to face her. "Elaine, what are you doing here? I didn't invite you."

She steps up to the bar by my side. "No, but Lance did."

"What do you want?" I ask, finally glancing at her for the first time.

She pouts. "That's not a nice way to talk to your baby sister, who you haven't seen in four years."

I shake my head. "There's a reason I haven't seen you."

Her face falls. "Did you think I wouldn't attend my own father's funeral?" she asks, her voice turning vulnerable.

I shake my head. "I don't know what I thought. I haven't seen or heard from you in four years since you ran off with that wolf." I narrow my eyes at her. "It's odd timing that you would show up now."

She crosses her arms over her chest. "What are you suggesting?"

"Here is your drink, sir," the bartender returns and places it down on the bar.

I nod in thanks, and she walks away, leaving us again. "I don't have time to argue, Elaine. I have to select a wife tonight." I knock back the bourbon in one, letting the cold liquid calm the anger burning inside of me.

She sets her hand on my arm, squeezing gently. "I don't want to argue, brother. I just want to make amends."

A tension coils through my muscles. "Why now, Elaine?"

She shrugs. "You're different from father. Can't you see past my mate?"

I run a hand through my hair, drawing in a deep breath. She's right. I am different from our father. Elaine mated young. She was eighteen years old when she met Luke, a wolf shifter. My father wanted them to break the bond, but they both refused. She ran away with him. I haven't heard from her since.

My father did threaten to kill Luke if he saw him again. It was one of the last things he said to his daughter. I can't deny that she must be hurting over it.

I nod my head. "Stay, and we will talk in the coming days," I say, not wanting to discuss it here and now.

I'm too wound up, not by her, but by Lance. It would be a terrible idea to have this conversation in front of all these people. Elaine and I often struggle to see eye to eye, even when we were children.

"Thank you," she says, her voice quiet.

I nod, patting her on the shoulder before turning and heading back toward the stage at the front.

It's time to get this evening over and done with. There's no chance in hell I'm picking a wife, so Lance will have to accept it.

I move through the crowd, tense, and on edge. My dragon is ready to break free, but I'm not sure why. A few scales break out across the skin at my wrist. The last thing I want tonight is to demonstrate that I'm not in control. Too many witnesses here that don't exactly like me.

A strong scent of strawberries hits me as I move forward, drawing my attention toward the opposite side of the ballroom. My heart skips a beat, and I feel the burning pull of my dragon trying to break free. He wants to rise to the surface, hence the scales.

It feels like time slows down as she gracefully walks down the steps into the ballroom. Her dark hair is long and falls in waves over her olive skin. I let my eyes drag down her form, feeling the pull of my dragon ramp up. Her hourglass figure and shapely curves do nothing to tame the blazing fire inside of me.

My cock is harder than a rock, straining against my tight boxer briefs. I'm staring at my mate. She isn't royalty—she isn't even a dragon shifter.

I know that from her scent. I focus on it, trying to work out precisely what she is. There's no way she's a wolf shifter. She smells too good. *Human?* I shake my head, knowing that's not it either.

I feel panic set in, as that only leaves a witch or a vampire. Both races are entirely off the table for dragon shifters, especially royalty.

As she gets closer to me, her eyes meet mine. A flash of fear enters her bright green gems. She recognizes me instantly, and she's worried.

Is she even supposed to be here?

I know no vampires are invited to this ball, but she doesn't have that undead scent either. It leaves one option—a witch. Some witches got an invitation here tonight, but only ones I'm formally acquainted with. I'm not acquainted with this stunning beauty.

She slips out of my sight quickly, trying to evade my gaze. It's a bad idea to try and evade my dragon when he's on heat. I feel the excitement at the chase build inside of me, and it's impossible to deaden. This woman is playing with fire if she doesn't play ball.

I smile as I catch a glimpse of her dress as she moves toward the bar. Many people underestimate a dragon's vision. It's second to none. I track her every movement as she settles in on a stool, clearly trying to blend in as best she can. Little does she know that she can't hide from me.

My dragon roars to break free. He loves a chase. I rein it in, clenching my fists and walking toward her. Finding my mate is the last thing I expected to happen tonight. My mate. A witch.

Fuck.

It's not entirely shocking. Lately, more and more species are mating with others outside of their own. Rhys, the wolf shifter king, has mated to a human and has children with her. I never once thought I'd see wolf shifter royalty take a human for a mate.

Sure, their royalty is a bit different from ours. Rhys doesn't live in a castle or have ridiculous wealth, but he's still the leader of all the wolves in North America.

I'm not sure I'm going to have quite the same freedom to take a witch as a mate. For a start, we're sworn enemies, other than the few witches that have changed sides and remain loyal to the dragons. Lance would kill me if I even suggested taking a witch as my wife.

Her scent calls to me as I move toward the bar. My

heartbeat picks up pace as I set eyes on her again. She has her back to me, leaning over the bar.

I take a moment to admire her from behind. She's perfect. Every single inch of her makes me harder than nails—her curvy figure and perfect, round ass.

I groan, trying to control the urges rearing up inside of me. There's no way I can stay away from her tonight. The princesses that came her to win me over won't get a fucking look from me—not now.

I'm ready to claim my mate, and so is my dragon. The claiming could cause a commotion, but I'm not about to turn my back on my mate to satisfy my people. She's mine, whether they like it or not.

4

ILSA

*H*is eyes remain fixed on me as I move across the ballroom floor. There's no mistaking who he is. The dragon king, Aiden Jeremiah, is staring right at me.

Does he know that I'm not supposed to be here?

Fuck

After being ambushed by Alena in the bathroom, and now him staring at me, I'm starting to think this night is destined to go wrong.

I try to slip out of his view, but it feels like his eyes follow me everywhere. This is the last thing I need. Sure, I want a moment of his time, but having him notice me before I had the chance to notice him has me on edge. Maybe the guards knew I was an imposter and fore-warned him.

I know what dragon shifters do to witches who they aren't allies with. They burn them to a crisp. I slip through the crowd, hoping the bar will be good cover from him. There are so many people. He'll surely lose sight of me, even with his hyper-vision.

I move toward the bar, slipping through people chatting. A drink is well deserved right now. My heart is hammering so fast. I'm sure I might suffer from cardiac arrest at any moment.

"What can I get you, sweetheart?" the bartender asks, flashing his sharp dragon teeth. It's not often I've been this close to a dragon, and it's unnerving.

I swallow hard, knowing how much danger I'm in right now. "Jack and Coke, please."

He winks. "Coming right up, beautiful."

Heat floods me at the compliment. If anyone were to realize I'm not supposed to be here, I could be torn apart in seconds. I keep my elbows propped against the bar, feeling my head spin. This was a bad idea. I feel like the lamb who has voluntarily walked into the wolves' den like a damn idiot.

A hand lands on my shoulder, making me jump.

I spin around and almost squeal when I see who is standing behind me. Aiden. His bright orange eyes are dragon-like. I'm sure he's about to turn and rip me to shreds. "Let me get that," he says, nodding at the other shifter.

The flirty bartender looks pale as he nods, setting the drink down in front of me.

"And, a bourbon on the rocks for me, Will," he says, glaring at the guy behind the bar.

He nods and goes to fetch the drink.

"What's your name?" Aiden asks. He stares at me with such intensity, and I feel my knees wobble.

I try to remember Alena's reassurance that Aiden isn't heartless like his father. He won't hurt me for the sake of it, I hope she's right.

I swallow hard and try to speak, but nothing comes out. The man standing in front of me is the single most attractive man I've ever seen.

Dragon shifters are so often painfully handsome, but his looks are on another level. He has high cheekbones and a strong jaw, peppered with a dark, neatly trimmed beard. His hair is jet black too, but the most striking thing about him are those eyes—piercing, fiery orange flecked with gold. His pupils are elongated, which warns me I'm in danger. A dragon shifter's eyes only look like that when their dragon is close to the surface.

His nostrils flare, and he steps closer to me, setting his hands down either side of the bar, trapping me between it and him. "I asked you a question," he murmurs.

His voice isn't threatening. Instead, it's seductive. My heart hammers against my rib cage. His scent over-whelms me. He smells of musk and the mountains—it's so masculine it makes my body quiver.

"Ilsa," I say, trying to compose myself.

Aiden is more than I expected and undeniably attractive. I can't explain the urge I have to grab him and kiss him. It makes no sense. It's forbidden for witches to get close to dragons, but it's all I can think about.

"Ilsa," he repeats my name, and hearing it on his lips turns me into molten lava. "I'm Aiden." He removes his hands from the bar, finally giving me some space. He holds out a hand for me to shake.

I stare at it for a moment, dazed. "I know who you are. Who doesn't?" I take his hand and shake it. "It's lovely to meet you, your highness."

He laughs at that. "Don't ever call me that again, it's just Aiden, love."

I can't understand why my stomach does a backflip at him calling me *love*. He probably calls every woman that, but it sounds sexy in his mild British accent. His family originally came from Britain but moved to the United States a while ago. He would have been born here but must have inherited it from his parents.

"Okay, Aiden," I say, trying to reclaim my hand from his tight grip.

He doesn't let it go. "What brings a stunning woman like you here tonight?" he asks.

I feel my mouth drop open, pretty sure I need to pick it up off the floor. Aiden, the king of dragons, is flirting with me. This has to be a trap. "I was invited," I say, swallowing the moment the lie leaves my lips.

He shakes his head. "No, you weren't. I know every witch who is invited, but I don't know you, unluckily enough for me." His eyes narrow. "I intend to right that tonight."

I try to pull my hand from his. "I will leave, please, don't hurt—"

He pulls me into his chest, suddenly, stopping me mid-sentence. "I'd never hurt you, Ilsa," he growls, voice low and deep. He looks overcome with desire. "I need to dance the first dance alone with a woman of my choosing. Would you do me the honor?"

I shake my head, trying to pull away. "That would be a terrible idea. I'm the worst dancer ever."

He lets go of my hand, but his eyes flash at my refusal. He looks even more determined. He's not going to let this go without a fight, but I cannot dance to save my life. I need to stay close to him to ask him about my family, but the idea of dancing in front of all these people makes me feel sick.

"I'll do all the work, and you trust me and follow my lead."

I raise a brow. "Are you asking me to trust a stranger?"

Considering Aiden is the king, his conduct isn't very royal. The last thing he should be doing is asking a random witch to dance the first dance with him. If rumors are to be believed, he's supposed to select a dragon shifter princess as a wife tonight.

I can't deny that the idea of him taking anyone else as a wife makes me jealous, which is crazy. I don't know this man.

He shrugs. "I'm asking you to let me lead you through this."

Indecision plagues me as I wonder whether this is a trap. The king can't want to dance with me. Although, it's impossible to ignore the desire in his eyes. I find myself drowning in them as I nod my head. "Fine, one dance, but don't say I didn't warn you."

He laughs a deep rumble that rocks me to my core. "Warn me about what?"

"How bad a dancer I am. Be prepared to be embarrassed."

He raises a brow. "That won't happen, I promise." He holds his hand out again.

I stare at it. This man could hold all the answers I need to find my family. I may hate dancing, but I know they would do the same for me. They would do anything to save me, and now I need to do anything to save them.

Slowly, I put my hand into his. I gasp, as a spark flows through my body, sending heat through every vein. Deep down, I know It's not the only reason I want to agree to dance with him. There's a connection between us—one I can't explain.

His eyes are fiery as he searches my face. I will feel so unbelievably inadequate, dancing with a man like him. He's stunning. I'm just an average witch—one that has never had any hope when it comes to dating. The way he is looking at me makes me feel like the only other person in the room—the only other person in the world.

I don't know why he's looking at me like that.

"Come on," he says, pulling me toward the dance floor.

I swallow hard and try to ignore my anxiety. I repeat the truth over and over in my head.

It's for my family.

I'll do anything to save them, even if it means putting my life in the hands of a dragon shifter.

Witches are naturally introverted, but I'm as bad as they get. I'm happy staying out of the limelight as much as possible.

Aiden comes to a stop in the middle of the dance floor and pulls me close to him. His arm wraps around my waist, and he hoists me against his hard chest. "Trust me, love," he utters.

My heart pounds frantically against my rib cage as I stare into his eyes. The heat increases and travels to my cheeks as he looks at me like he wants to devour me. It's a look that would scare most people, considering he's a dragon. For some reason, it doesn't scare me. It has the opposite effect.

He gives me a reassuring nod. "Don't worry. Follow my lead."

He's talking about dancing like royalty, and I have no clue how. Somehow, the look in his eyes tells me everything will be alright. This man I don't know will catch me if I fall.

He pushes me away slightly, keeping his right hand higher up on my back and taking my right hand in his left. A beat comes from somewhere, and I know it's about to start.

"Ready?" he asks.

I shake my head. There's no way I could ever be ready for this. My knees wobble slightly as the anticipation only increases my anxiety about dancing in front of everyone. I might be kicked for ruining the king's first dance after this, anyway.

5

AIDEN

*M*y hand remains tightly entwined with hers as I lead her onto the dance floor. It's time for the first dance, which the king must always open alone. Lance won't like it, but I've found the woman I'm spending this night with. I've found the woman I'm spending the rest of my life with, even if she doesn't realize it yet.

She's aroused. I can sense it in her movements. The way her lips keep parting temptingly every time I get close or touch her. I can scent it too. It's damn well intoxicating and a miracle I'm keeping the reins on my dragon right now. He wants out. He wants to claim.

I want to spend this night making sure this beauty has the best time possible. She looked uneasy when she first stepped into the ballroom, but on my arm, she seems at ease.

Perhaps because she knows deep down, I'd never let

anyone hurt her. I know she isn't supposed to be here. She isn't one of the witches we have on our side.

I walk her into the center of the ballroom and come to a stop, pulling her close to me. She tenses in my arms for a moment before relaxing. "Trust me, love," I whisper into her ear, trying to ease her anxiety.

She stares into my eyes. There's a mix of fear and desire in her emerald gems. I wish she knew there was nothing to fear, not when she's with me.

I give her a nod. "Don't worry. Follow my lead."

Ilsa looks terrified as I push her away slightly. As king, I have to follow certain etiquette. It's archaic if you ask me, but I have no choice but to follow the rules. My right-hand settles higher up on her back, and I take her right hand in my left.

The beats come, counting down to the start of the music and dance. It's right on time, as always.

"Ready?" I ask, squeezing her hand softly.

She shakes her head, making me laugh.

"Tough," I say.

The music starts, and I swiftly pull her into a waltz across the clearing of the dance floor.

Her eyes are wide as she desperately tries to keep her footsteps moving at the same speed. Within moments, she finds her rhythm. "I hate that everyone is watching us."

I shake my head. "Everyone is watching you, love. You are stunning."

She doesn't take the compliment well, as a grimace flashes across her face.

"Did I say something wrong?"

She shakes her head. "No, it's just this dress isn't mine, it's—"

"I wasn't talking about the dress. I'm talking about the woman in it." I twirl her around, pulling her back into my chest and swaying. "You could be naked, and you'd be just as stunning, in fact, probably more." I twirl her back away. "I wish you had come naked."

Her cheeks turn red at my shameless flirting, and she falls silent.

Damn.

Maybe I pushed too hard too soon. As I twirl Ilsa back toward me, I let my hand wander slightly lower on her back. She turns an even darker red. "Sorry for being a bit forward, but you drive me crazy."

Her brow furrows. "Is that a line you use on every woman?"

Rage coils through me at the suggestion I'd be interested in any other woman. She's my mate. I take a deep breath, trying to calm down. I need to remember that she's a witch. She may be my mate, but witches don't have mates. She may feel a connection, but it won't be as deep as what I feel for her. It never could be. "No."

I twirl her away and then pull her back to me, leaning her over at the finale. Claps surround us from the other party guests, and they begin to join in for the second dance.

"You are a great dancer. I'm not sure what you were worried about." I link my hands with hers and pull her off the dance floor. "There's something I want to show you."

She yanks me to a stop, pulling her hand away. "Where are we going?"

It's impossible not to note the suspicion in her tone and eyes. She doesn't trust me, and that hurts for some silly reason. I know she doesn't feel this the way I do. I force a smile. "It's a surprise, trust me, love." I hold my hand out to her.

Her eyes flash again when I call her that, but she's quick to accept, entwining her fingers with mine.

I pull her through the crowd. Hundreds of eyes are on us—all of them judging us. The king shouldn't be spending so much time with a female witch, particularly at a ball set up for him to select a wife. The rumor mill will be in overdrive by the morning. I can't find it in me to care as I tighten my grip on my mate's hand.

We slip out of the ballroom, and I turn right, heading toward the library. I want some time alone with Ilsa to explain to her what this is.

"Are you not going to tell me where we are going?" she asks, eyes on me.

I glance at her. "Somewhere private," I murmur, unable to hide the huskiness from my voice.

She bites her bottom lip, and her cheeks turn a deeper pink. I'm glad she doesn't question me anymore as I make it to the library. I open the door and pull her inside.

Her eyes go wide as she twirls around, looking in awe at the room. It's an impressive room. The walls are lined from floor to ceiling in books. "Wow, that's a lot of books."

I smile as I watch her move toward one of the bookcases, brushing her fingers lightly over the spines.

"Do you like to read?" I ask.

She glances back at me. "I used to, but lately, I never get the time." Our eyes meet for a long time in silence, and the tension rises between us. It feels like she sees right into my soul with those stunning green eyes.

"What brought you here tonight, Ilsa?" I ask.

She tenses visibly, breaking eye contact, and looking back at the books. "What do you mean?" Her voice is shaky, and I can smell the fear tinging the air.

"I mean, I know you are gatecrashing this party. There's a reason you are here, isn't there?"

She spins around, pressing her back into the bookcase. "Look, I don't want any trouble. I just have some questions." The fear has overtaken, and her pupils have dilated.

I shake my head. "I'm not going to hurt you, love. Come on." I nod my head toward a sofa in front of a fireplace.

She moves cautiously toward it and takes a seat.

I click my fingers, lighting the logs in the hearth.

Ilsa's gaze doesn't leave me for a moment. She's turned defensive as she keeps her arms crossed over her chest.

I take a seat next to her, gently setting my hand on her knee.

She shifts away, but it's impossible to ignore the way her heart rate picks up.

My dragon excites at the pattering beat flooding the air. He wants her aroused and on edge, ready for him to claim. I grit my teeth, trying to ignore the filthy thoughts racing through my mind. All I can do is picture her butt naked and ready for me.

"You can tell me why you came. I have no intention of hurting you."

Intrigue ignites in her eyes as she glances from me to the blazing fire in front of us. She shivers.

"Are you cold?" I ask

She shakes her head. "No, just on edge."

I set my hand on her knee again, and this time, she doesn't pull away. "Don't be."

She swallows and meets my gaze. "I'm here to find out the truth about my family's disappearance." Pain flits across her face. "They went missing two days before your father's death. The same day my brother went to meet with your father." She draws in a deep breath. "They never returned."

Fuck.

My father was an evil son of a bitch when it came to witches and warlocks, but I wouldn't expect him to break her brother's trust at a meeting if he agreed on a meeting. "My father wouldn't hurt a warlock he had invited to a meeting." I shake my head. "He could be brutal at times, but not that brutal." At least, I hope not. My father often felt I was weak. If he had been luring witches under false pretenses to the castle, he wouldn't have told me.

Disappointment flits onto her face. "What explanation is there for their disappearance?"

I shake my head. "I don't know, but I'll help you find out."

Her eyes widen. "You will? Why?"

I swallow hard, knowing I need to tell her the truth. Keeping the fact that she's my mate from her helps nothing. "I assume you know about fated mates for shifters."

The puzzled look on her face tells me she isn't anticipating what I'm about to reveal to her. I'd hoped deep down, maybe she knew. "Yes, what's that got to do with you helping me?" she asks, searching my eyes for the answer.

Worry grips at my heart. I'm a total stranger to her. If she freaks out, then it could test the already weak bond between us. I grab her hand and squeeze. "Ilsa, it has everything to do with me helping you."

I hope she might grasp it herself, but she stares at me blankly. It's now or never. There's no way I want to watch her walk away tonight—I'm not sure I could. "You're my fated mate."

She laughs at that as if I'm joking. "Don't be ridiculous. I'm a witch, and you're a dragon shifter king."

I feel pain grip my chest at her refusal to accept the

truth. My dragon, on the other hand, only feels uncontrollable rage. The rage takes over all other emotions—it always does.

I clench my fists by my side and stand. The best thing to do right now is pace the floor, channeling the rage anywhere but at Ilsa. I don't want to scare her, but I don't feel in control right now.

It's hard at times controlling the beastly part of myself.

"Aiden?" Ilsa says my name, and it draws my eyes back to her.

The moment I set eyes on her, I feel my control slip. He's ready to claim. I shake my head. "It's not a joke, Ilsa. You don't know what you are talking about. My dragon can recognize our soul mate, or are you questioning that?"

I hate the anger in my voice and the way she pales. It's impossible to control, particularly around her. She brings the beast to the surface so fucking quickly.

She sinks back into the sofa, almost shrinking.

I shake my head. "Sorry, I'm struggling to control myself around you." I step toward the sofa, but she stands and backs away. The fear in her eyes cuts me to the core. "Please, Ilsa, listen to me."

She glances down at her dress, which is starting to change color from white and gold to black. "I've got to get out of here."

I watch as she spins around and starts to run from me. My dragon urges me to follow, and I can't resist the pull of chasing my mate. It's primal and archaic, and it drives me wild.

She flings open the doors and disappears into the corridor.

I follow her, surprised how quick she is for a witch. I'm so fixated on her that I don't see Charles in my path. "Wow, Aiden, where are you going in such a hurry?" He holds his hands up to stop me, but I knock him out of the way. My dragon only has one thing on his mind right now.

Ilsa should be easy for me to catch, but she's already disappeared into the crowd ahead. I curse under my breath and break into a fast sprint, using my senses to track her. There's no way we are letting her get away.

6

ILSA

I almost trip over my own feet as I rush down the castle steps.

Aiden is in pursuit. "Ilsa, wait."

My heart is hammering as I rush away from the man that just told me I'm his mate. Aiden is a complication that I can't deal with. Even if he could help me find my family, they have to remain my sole focus. Not to mention, my dress has entirely changed back now to the little black dress I had on before.

"Please," he shouts, catching me up.

"No, Aiden, please leave me alone." I can feel tears welling in my eyes, but I'm not sure why. It hurts, running from him, which makes no sense. I've just met the guy—a man who is totally and utterly off-limits.

"I can't." He grabs my hand, forcing me to a stop. "I would do anything for you. Tell me what you need help with, and I'll do it."

I search the eyes of the shifter who insists he's my mate. "We've just met. Why would you do anything?"

"I told you, Ilsa, you are my mate. My soul mate." He pulls me toward him and cups my face. "Let me prove it to you."

His eyes are blazing with a need that makes my thighs clench. I feel my lips part involuntarily, thinking about him kissing me—this god of a man.

He moves closer, and his lips meet mine. A spark of pure lust rushes through me the moment our lips touch. He runs his hands to my hips, gripping hard.

I feel his tongue probing at my lips, requesting entrance. It's as if I'm powerless to resist as I let him in. I moan as his tongue tangles with mine. My body is turning to jelly in his arms. I let my hands move to his hard chest, feeling his muscles beneath his shirt. The dragon king shouldn't be touching me, let alone kissing me.

All I can focus on is how good it makes me feel. I want this man more than I've ever wanted anyone or anything in my life.

How can this be happening?

I came here to find the truth about my family's disappearance. He promises to help me, but what if it's a trap—a trap to capture me too. Maybe Aiden knows where they are. I can't be Aiden's fated mate. It's not possible.

He tightens his grip on me, pulling me harder against him and growling against my lips. "It is possible. I'd never hurt you, Ilsa," he murmurs against my lips.

I shake my head. "This can't work… You know it's forbidden."

He digs his fingertips harder into my hips. "It has to work because you're mine, love," he breathes, moving his lips to my neck and kissing me there. "Mine forever."

A shudder pulses through me as I dig my fingertips into his hard biceps. His body presses into mine, commanding me. He towers over me and is a wall of pure muscle. I want him with every fiber of my being.

Someone clearing their throat behind us has us both jumping apart. "Your majesty. What are you doing?" the man asks.

Aiden's eyes flash with pure rage. "Are you questioning your king?" he growls.

The shifter at the top of the stairs pales and shakes his head. "No, I'm your royal advisor, and I'm advising you to stop what you are doing right now if you care about your future as king."

Aiden's muscles strain, and his eyes burn even more brightly with rage. "Lance, I'm the king, and I will do whatever the hell I want. If you want to challenge me, then challenge me." He marches toward him, looming over the guy.

Lance shakes his head. "You know that's not what I meant. She's a witch." He glances at me.

Aiden snaps and grabs his arms, forcing Lance's

attention back on him. "She's my mate. Do you understand?"

Lance is so pale he looks like a ghost. "Your mate?" he repeats.

"Yes, my fucking mate. Do you still want to challenge me?" he growls.

I walk up the steps and set a hand on his arm. "Aiden, calm down."

He snaps around, making me jump, but the moment our eyes meet, the rage dissipates.

Lance glances at me and gives me a small nod of thanks. "I'm sorry for interrupting you, sir, please forgive me." He bows low and then backs away.

Aiden doesn't even look his way; let alone say anything in reply. His eyes focus on me, and it makes me tremble. The intensity of his gaze sends my mind reeling. All I can think about is ripping his shirt off and worshipping his chiseled body.

What the hell is wrong with me

This is ridiculous, as we've only just met. I don't know this man at all. The look in his eyes tells me I should run away. He's dangerous, aggressive, and a fucking dragon shifter. Witches and dragons don't mix— not in that way.

Once we're alone again, he steps forward and circles my waist with his arm. "Come with me. I want to show you something," he breathes.

I swallow hard, before nodding. The last thing I should be doing is agreeing to go anywhere with Aiden.

I've just witnessed the rage he harbors inside. Dragons are renowned for being angry creatures.

He entwines his hand with mine and leads me down the steps and to the left of the castle.

We walk in uneasy silence. "Where are we going?" I ask.

He smiles. "Do you want to go for a ride, love?"

I raise a brow, dirty thoughts rising to the surface of my mind. "What kind of ride?"

"One you'll never forget." He nods over to a gate. "Go stand over there."

I'm hesitant, but I do as he says.

My heart starts to hammer as he begins to unbutton his shirt—heat pulses through my body. A shudder races through me. I want to see him naked, but I'm not sure why he is stripping right here. "W-What are you doing?" I ask.

He smiles. "Don't worry. It's not what you think." He chucks his shirt down on the floor, before moving his fingers to his belt.

My mouth goes dry as I let my eyes roam every dip and ridge of his muscular chest and abdomen. I can feel the desire pooling inside of me. An insatiable hunger to walk toward him and worship his body.

Despite him insisting this isn't what I think, I want it to be. He throws his belt down before chucking his pants on top of the pile. His cock is hard and bulging against the fabric of his boxer briefs, making me so wet. I take a step toward him without thinking.

He grits his teeth and holds his hand up. "No, love, stay there."

My knees shake as he hooks his finger into the waist-band of his boxer briefs. An involuntary whimper escapes my mouth as the desire builds inside of me.

Aiden smirks, before pulling them down.

I gasp as his huge, thick cock bobs out of his pants. My body turns to molten lava, and it takes all my willpower to stay where I am. I lick my lips, feeling my mouth water at the idea of tasting him.

He groans softly. "I'm going to shift and take you for a ride," he says, snapping me out of my daze. "Climb on my back once I've shifted."

His words sober me, snapping me out of the lust-filled daze I'd fallen into. I keep my eyes off the consid-erable package between his thighs and nod. Unsure how I feel about climbing onto a dragon's back.

He roars softly as red scales start to burst over every inch of his skin.

My heart pounds at a hundred miles an hour as his form begins to grow and change. It's mind-blowing the way his body morphs into a vast, beautiful dragon. Once he is standing in his dragon form, his eyes meet mine. The same eyes I saw him look at me with when he held me close.

He cocks his head as a sign to get on.

I swallow hard and step toward him. Once I reach him, I run my hand across the smooth red scales.

He makes a low rumbling noise when my hands

touch him. Aiden kneels lower, with one wing spread to allow me to climb onto his back. I hesitate for a moment, but deep down, I know it's safe.

I climb onto his back, straddling his neck.

I panic the moment he stands, realizing I've got nothing to hold on to. My heart is pounding hard and fast against my rib cage.

Without warning, he launches into the sky with his sturdy legs and begins to lift higher until we're above the valley where his castle sits.

I don't look down. Heights aren't exactly a strong point for me. Instead, I keep my eyes forward as he plunges over the mountains. I grip onto his neck as best I can, holding on for my life.

The stars and moon twinkle brightly overhead, lighting our path. My heart skips a beat as I notice the sparkling surface of Lake Tahoe. It's beautiful under the glowing light of the moon. My fear begins to ease as I stare out over the expanse of water.

Aiden dips down suddenly, skating across the surface of the water with expert precision. It's exhilarating—the feeling of flying so freely, being one with nature. I feel a small amount of envy that Aiden can shift and fly wherever and whenever he wants. It must feel amazing to have that ability.

He pulls up into the air and flies around a bend in the mountain, heading into a small bay with a beach. Suddenly he lets fire rip from his mouth, lighting the water. The heat is immense. I'm not sure what he's doing, but the water bubbles as he keeps setting flames over it.

After a few minutes of him burning the water with the fire, he heads for the beach and lands. He sets his wing down again, and I climb off, feeling my heels sink into the sand.

I quickly take them off and set them to the side. When I turn back around, Aiden is standing behind me in his human form. The moon emphasizes every curve and dip of his muscles. I can't help my eyes wander down his body to his huge erection still hard and jutting out from between his thighs.

"Like what you see, love?" he asks, snapping my eyes back up to his.

I swallow hard and force my eyes to the lake, staring over the sparkling surface of it. "It's beautiful out here. Why did you breathe fire over the water?" I ask.

He approaches me and stands by my side. "So we could go for a swim." He smirks. "It will be nice and warm now."

I raise a brow. "I don't have a swimsuit."

He shrugs. "Neither do I. Strip," he orders.

The way he says it makes my body heat. It's insane the effects this man has on me. I turn around and glance over my shoulder. "I'll need help."

His eyes flash with desire as his hand moves to unzip my dress from the back. I feel his skin tease against the nape of my neck as he brushes my hair out of the way.

Aiden slowly undoes the zip, letting my dress fall to my hips.

I move to pull it down, but he stops me, doing it himself.

A deep groan escapes his lips, making my heart rate pick up. I spin around and stare at him. His lips quirk up into a smirk as his eyes drag down my half-naked body. "Stunning," he murmurs.

Heat flushes my cheeks and spreads through my body.

"Now the underwear," he orders.

I swallow hard and shake my head. "I'll wear them in."

He raises a brow. "What will you wear after our swim then?" Aiden asks, setting his hands on my bare waist.

It feels like his touch shocks me. I'm too weak to resist him. Instead, I launch myself into his arms and kiss him hard, feeling right again once my lips are on his.

His tongue swipes through my mouth desperately, sending need pulsing between my thighs.

I dig my fingertips into his hair, wanting to claw him closer.

He flicks open the clasp on my bra at my back and swipes it away from me, stepping back to get a look.

I feel suddenly self-conscious and cover my breasts with my hands.

"Don't cover yourself," he growls.

I slowly peel my hands away and free my breasts.

His eyes darken and dilate more. The elongated pupils are getting thicker. "Panties off, now," he says, stepping closer to me again.

I hook my fingers into them, knowing I can't deny him anything, not now.

His eyes track my movements as I pull them down, exposing myself to him. He comes at me like a man possessed, pulling me into his body. Our mouths meet in a desperate and frantic kiss as his hands search every inch of me.

I gasp as he lifts me into his arms, carrying me toward the water. "Are you sure it's going to be warm?" I ask, eyeing the sparkling liquid he's about to plunge us in.

"Positive, trust me, love." He walks into the water and sets me down.

My eyes widen at how warm the water is. It's probably the same temperature as a bath. "Wow, that's a pretty cool trick you've got."

He smiles the most beautiful smile I've ever seen. "Yeah, it only lasts so long, though."

Our eyes stay locked on each other as he starts to move forward. It's an oddly freeing feeling, skinny dipping in such a secluded place under the stars, particularly with him.

He grabs my hand and pulls me against him.

I moan as his hard cock settles against my tummy. "What are you doing?"

"Claiming what is mine," he murmurs, kissing my neck.

I moan as he moves his hands down my hips to cup my ass. I should leave, but I can't resist his touch.

"I don't understand," I say, despite leaning into his hard, muscular body. My mind and mouth are protesting pathetically, but my body is in this one-hundred percent.

"Don't fight your instincts, Ilsa." His hand trails between my thighs, making me pant for breath. It feels like I'm so hot I'm going to explode at any moment. "I know you want this as much as I do."

He trails hot, passionate kisses down the center of my chest.

I lace my fingers in his thick, brown hair as his lips clamp around my nipples, making them even harder than they already are. My pussy is dripping wet as he moves his hands down to cup me there.

"So wet," he murmurs.

I gasp as his thick finger dips inside of me, making my heart rate double in speed. I'm doing this with a dragon, which is so wrong. Nothing has ever felt so right in my life, though. We're natural enemies, and yet all I feel for this man is desire.

I dig my fingertips into his hard biceps, trying to steady myself as he kisses my neck and shoulders. My body shakes as he sinks his teeth softly into my skin, sending a thrilling sting through my nerves.

He moves his finger in and out of me slowly, teasingly, before pulling out and rubbing my clit.

My head falls back as his fingers work me into a frenzy. "Aiden," I gasp his name as he moves, he bends down to suck on my tender, hard nipples.

I can't believe we're doing this out in the open. We may be in the middle of nowhere, but this is dragon shifter territory. They can fly anywhere. The only reprieve is that most of them are at the castle right now.

I moan as he tightens his grip on my hips, making me needier.

He slips another thick finger inside of me, pumping them in and out at increased tempo. Aiden seems to know how to hit the exact right spot deep inside of me.

I arch my back as he pushes me higher and higher, his cock throbbing between us. My hand circles his thick shaft, and I tug, feeling the need inside of me grow more intense.

He growls a deep sound as I continue to pump my hand up and down his shaft, finding my fingers barely wrap around him.

The thought of having him inside of me makes me wild. I'm not usually so reckless with someone I barely know, and yet, I can't even reason with myself right now.

Aiden pushes me backward toward a rock in the water and perches me on it, spreading my legs. I heat as his gaze darkens, staring at my pussy.

He moves forward and sets his lips on my inner thigh, sending a shiver right up my spine.

I lace my wet fingers into his hair as his mouth moves closer to my center.

His hot breath teases the sensitive, wet folds. Aiden teases me, letting his breath fall on my aching clit. The need to feel his mouth on me increasing every second that ticks past.

"Please, Aiden," I gasp.

He smirks at me. "Begging already, love?" he asks, eyes sparkling in the dim light of the moon and stars.

"Yes." I nod my head. "Please, I need to feel you."

His eyes dilate even more as he fists his cock in his hand and presses his tongue against my aching clit.

I jolt at the sudden contact of his tongue as he starts to lick me. His tongue flicks between my clit and my folds expertly, sending me higher and higher. I lace my fingers in his hair, trying to get more from him.

He brings his fingers back to my pussy and thrusts them inside, still licking me. It's intense and all-consuming as he pushes me toward the edge of no return. The sight of the powerful, dragon king kneeling before me and licking me, while stroking his cock is the single most arousing thing I've seen in my life.

He pulls away briefly. "Fuck you taste like honey," he growls, before licking me more.

My vision starts to blur as Aiden doesn't give me a moments reprieve, pushing me toward breaking point as he curls his fingers inside of me.

I cry out, feeling my orgasm break at that moment. It's intense and overwhelming. Every muscle in my body tenses, and my pussy clamps down around his fingers. "Fuck, Aiden," I moan.

Aiden keeps licking my clit, before removing his fingers and lapping up every drop of my juice. He licks his fingers once he's done, holding my gaze.

I watch as he stands. His chiseled chest and abs sparkling as the moonlight hits the rivulets of water running off him. My mouth waters as his cock becomes visible, but by the look on his face, he has no intention of letting me taste him.

He grabs me off the rock and kisses me slow and deep. "It's late. We should head back to the castle."

"What time is it?" I ask, glancing around for some sort of indication.

He shrugs. "It's the early hours of the morning. The birds are already singing."

I pause and listen, realizing he is right. "Yes, we best get back," I say, knowing that if I stay here with him any longer, I'll do something I regret.

This already went too far between us tonight. There's an unspoken tension between us. We both know that witches and dragons don't fit.

He lifts me and carries me back to shore, making my heart speed up.

I want to tell him I can walk myself, but then, for once in my life, I feel cared for in a way I never thought I'd find. Allowing someone else to look after me is a luxury I wish to indulge in for a moment.

Aiden sets me down on the sandy bank of the bay and watches me intently. "Getting dressed is optional." He raises a brow. "I can fly you straight back to my room."

There's a promise in his tone, and it sets my belly on fire.

I shake my head. "I'll dress and head back to town. I can't stay."

Disappointment flares in his eyes as he watches me grab my clothes and throw them on. I turn around and glance at him. "Can you zip me up?" I ask.

He nods and steps forward, jaw clenched tightly. "Of course." His fingers brush my skin before he zips up the dress slowly.

I turn around once it's fastened.

"Ready?" he asks.

I nod and watch in awe as he shifts into his magnificent red dragon form. It's a beautiful sight to behold. I climb onto his back and keep my legs tight around him as he launches into the air.

This time feels more exhilarating, knowing what to expect. Aiden's massive wings beat the air as he speeds us back over the mountains and toward the castle. Within a couple of minutes, he touches down where we'd taken off in the castle gardens. His clothes remain in a pile on the floor.

He steps toward me, ignoring the clothes.

I gasp as he pulls me into him and kisses me hard. His body melds with mine. When he pulls back, we're both breathless. "Stay with me tonight," he murmurs into my ear softly.

My urges to be with him make me want to agree, but this is ridiculous. If I stay on this path, I'll get burned—literally.

7

AIDEN

*M*y heart aches as I watch her drive away. I know it's not goodbye, as she's given me her number, but my dragon wants to claim her now. It was fucking hard to let her leave.

She's distrusting of our kind in general. It's understandable since her family vanished after her brother met with my father. I wish I knew why—I wish I had the answers she is seeking, but I don't.

My position might make it easier for me to discover the truth. I'll do anything to win her over.

Who would have thought I'd be destined to mate to a witch?

It's uncommon for two siblings to mate to other species, particularly royal siblings. Perhaps Elaine and I have finally found common ground. We're both mated to species we're not supposed to be.

I turn around and walk up the steps of my castle, thankful to see that most of the guest's vehicles are gone.

Any of the princesses Lance invited here will be staying the night. Royal families are expected to host other royal families, but the rest of the guests should have left.

As I open the door to the castle, it seems eerily quiet. Lance is nowhere to be seen. Maybe he believes I've run away for good, as he usually always waits for my return. Lance has been in charge of my protection and training as a royal since I can remember.

I glance at the clock to see it's five in the morning. Lance may be dedicated, but perhaps it was pushing it to expect he'd still be up now.

I fling my jacket onto a chair in the hallway, before heading toward the stairs.

A scream catches me off guard.

What the fuck was that?

I race up the stairs searching for the source of the scream. Another piercing scream fills the air, and it's coming straight from my sister's room. "Elaine?" I shout her name, rounding the corner, and barreling into the door.

It's locked, but I put all my weight behind it, knocking it off the hinges. The sight in front of me floods me with deep horror—blood is all over the beige carpets and the cream, silk bedding.

A man is standing over my sister, holding a blood coated knife.

"What the fuck?"

I see red, charging for the guy. My vision tunnels,

and my body tenses as I feel my dragon rising to the surface. I miss the two other guys standing on the other side of the room in my state of pure panic and rage.

Elaine glances over at me, eyes wide. "Aiden, watch out," she mutters, but it's too late.

I turn in time for one of them to stab me in the gut. I growl at the pain, feeling myself shift anyway. It was too late to stop my transformation. His eyes go wide as I burn him to a crisp, catching the other guy also. It's not long until I burn him to ashes as well.

All I can feel is an all-consuming rage.

My heart pounds as I turn around to see my sister staring at me with wide eyes. The guy is kneeling over her still. He smirks as he knows I can't burn him. If I burn him, I kill Elaine along with him.

He twirls the knife around, tilting his head to the side. "What now?"

I growl at him, but I know there's nothing I can do, other than rush for him. My dragon is out of control as he does precisely that. The guy thrusts the knife into Elaine's heart, forcing me to a stop as I watch the life leave her eyes. My sister.

I feel all my grip on my human side snap as I launch myself at him, grabbing him with my talons and ripping him in two. Blood goes everywhere, but I don't care. My eyes go to Elaine's lifeless body. Her eyes are still full and open. Pain tears through me as I remember the way I spoke to her earlier. I didn't make amends.

The patter of footsteps heading my way catches my

attention. Ten guys all dressed in black and wearing balaclavas come in, cornering me.

What the fuck is this

This was an ambush—an attempt to wipe out the rest of the royal family in one swoop.

I feel the fire rising in my chest, but even for a dragon, there are too many armed attackers for me to overcome. Instead, my mind goes to survival. I focus solely on the French patio doors onto the balcony, launching across the room at it. The men shout, and a few let off rounds of bullets, but they bounce off my scales.

I growl as I launch myself through the glass, bounding onto the balcony. Blood rushes in my ears as I bound over the balustrade, dropping downward before swooping into the air.

They shoot at me from the balcony, but the only way to stop me would be to shift and chase me.

The pain in my stomach increases as I fly over the mountains. Blood drips from the knife wound in my stomach. I don't know where I'm going, but it feels like my dragon knows. My dragon's mind focuses on one thing—locating our mate.

She's the only one that can help. Tahoe City is a seventeen-mile flight from my castle, which in normal circumstances, would be easy. With a gut wound, I'm not sure I'll make it.

My hyper sensitive vision is blurred as I weave over the mountains and then drop down to skim over the lake. The water on my feet helps soothe me, but I know that my dragon is quickly losing strength.

Ilsa's face is clear in my mind. She's my savior. I need to get to her, no matter what. She's in Tahoe City. If I get there, I'll be able to find her. The question is whether or not I can make it without passing out.

I roar as I fly upward and scope out the distance, knowing I'm still a good few miles from the city. The light glistens on the edge of the water up ahead, but it's far.

People won't be too impressed if a dragon lands in the middle of their city. I'm going to have to land outside and then shift back to my human form, making the rest of my trip stark naked.

Humans are so funny about people walking around naked, but it's natural for shifters. We can't wear clothes when we shift.

I notice a spot on a hill overlooking the city, selecting it as the perfect spot. At least I'll have a downhill walk to Ilsa. My dragon can sense her already as my wings beat harder and faster. It feels like she's the only thing that can save me now. A witch has healing powers, but can she heal me?

The rumors are that witches are getting weaker and weaker as time goes on. Their numbers are reducing and they have no central coven, which weakens them further. She's my best hope, though.

I touch down on the soft grass of the hill, feeling my

knees wobble beneath me. My dragon is exhausted and shifting when injured can be dangerous.

I grit my teeth, growling lowly as I shift back into my human form. My body shakes, and I crash to the ground. A flood of weakness rushes through me. The wound is deep. I clutch my stomach, feeling the overwhelming pain increase in my human form.

Shit.

In dragon form, I have a much higher pain threshold. I keep my hand pressed against the bleeding cut in my abdomen and force myself to my feet. There are a few inns Ilsa could be staying at, but once I get closer, I hope I will scent her.

Clenching my fists, I force one foot in front of the other down the hill. My mind wanders as I make the short trek into the city.

I can't believe my sister is dead. I should have made amends with her, and now she'll never know that I didn't care who her mate was, and I never did. All I cared about was her happiness. I should have stood up to our father, but it's too late for that. Both of them are gone, and now I'm alone in this world.

Ilsa is all I've got left. She's my world. I won't watch her drive away again. She's never getting away from me. Life is too short, and I'm about to seize the reins and take what I want.

I stumble over a rock in the dark, twisting my ankle. The weakness is spreading to every part of me, including my eyesight. I usually can see through the night with no trouble, but it's growing increasingly difficult.

My ankle aches as I force myself to stand. I'm not falling at the last hurdle. The city is in my sights. I move faster down the hill, ignoring the splintering pain in my ankle and stomach.

Whoever attacked me at the castle, will be searching for me. It wasn't a random attack, not so soon after my father's murder.

I feel relief flood me as I make the last dash toward the edge of town. Now, I just need to find where Ilsa is staying. It can't be too hard.

8

ILSA

a hard bang comes at my door, making me jump. I sit bolt upright in bed, rubbing a hand across the back of my neck.

Who the fuck could that be?

I've paid up for three nights with the inn owner, so it can't be him. No one knows I'm staying here.

The knock comes again, harder. "Ilsa, please open the door."

I feel my heart in my throat at the sound of Aiden on the other side. He sounds like he's in pain.

I can't move quickly enough as I jump off the bed and rush for the door. My heart pounds against my rib cage at the thought of seeing him again. A dread twists my gut at why he's in pain. I open the door, hastily.

Aiden falls forward into my room entirely naked, crashing onto the floor.

My eyes widen at the blood covering his hands as he clutches his stomach.

"Aiden, what the hell happened?" I ask, shutting the door quickly in case whoever hurt him is still out there.

He shakes his head. "She's dead." Tears pool in his eyes.

I move his hand from the wound, finding the source of all the blood. It's a deep knife wound. "Who did this to you?" I put pressure on the wound, knowing that I need to seal it with magic. He's already lost too much blood. It will take a lot of my power to do it, but I know I have to. Aiden could die if I don't heal him.

"I don't know." He shakes his head. "Some people broke in. She's dead," Aiden says, voice cracking with emotion.

I squeeze his hand. "Who's dead?" I ask.

The tears flow down his face. "My sister, Elaine."

"I'm so sorry, Aiden." I grab his hand and squeeze before urging him to lie down flat. "Lie down. I need to patch you up, as you've lost too much blood, even for a dragon shifter."

He grunts as he lets his head rest back against the bedroom carpet.

"Hold still." I shut my eyes at first and hold my hands over the knife wound. I start to chant the healing spell under my breath, focusing all my energy into sealing the deep wound. "Et ad sanandum potentiam magia," I chant over and over again. The magic flares to life, and my eyes snap open, as magic floods into the cut.

He groans as the magic flares over his skin. His jaw is hard-set, and his fists clench by his side. Healing isn't exactly a painless experience for either party.

It's not easy for a witch to patch up a dragon with magic since it's draining—especially a witch with no coven. I may have one in principle, but it doesn't feel like it anymore. Our numbers are so low that our powers are waning day by day.

I continue to focus, keeping my eyes glued to the injury. The skin is almost entirely closed over. My powers feel like they are zapping every ounce of energy from my body. I sag to the side as I stop using my powers, feeling my head spin.

Aiden instinctively goes to grab me as I feel myself falling toward the floor. "Are you okay?" he asks, wincing as he moves to sit up.

"You shouldn't be asking me that question." I stare into his orange eyes, feeling that heat from earlier prickle across my body. Despite the exhausted condition I'm in, my mind goes to one thing whenever he is close. "I need you to help me get you over to the bed." I grab his arm and sling it over my shoulder, trying to help him up from the floor.

Aiden winces as he stands to his feet. The wound appears healed, but what I did was unnatural. He'll be in pain for a while and drained from the amount of blood he has lost. He leans on me with most of his weight as we stagger toward the bed.

He sits down, resting his face in his hands. The

tension in his shoulders is visible, and his breathing is heavy and labored.

I sit next to him and place a hand on his shoulder. "What happened?" I ask.

He shakes his head. "People were in the castle when I got back, and they killed my sister in front of my eyes, before trying to kill me."

"They almost succeeded." I set a hand down on his knee and squeeze. "How did you get here?"

He meets my gaze for the first time since he stood. "Shifted. I flew with the injury, but it took a lot out of me."

My brow furrows. "How did you know I was here?" I shake my head. "I didn't tell you…"

He raises a brow as if that's a stupid question. "You're my mate. I sensed you from your scent."

My eyes widen. The thought that Aiden can track me from my scent is a little unnerving. It means he could find me wherever I go.

He swallows hard. "I never got a chance to make amends with my sister."

My heart aches for him as I shift to pull him into a hug. I'm not sure what amends he needed to make, but I can hear the pain in his voice. "I'm so sorry, Aiden."

He pulls back and cups my face in his hands. "Don't be. You saved my life." He glances around the room. "Are you happy for me to stay the night?"

I nod my head immediately. "Of course, there's enough space for both of us." I stand, wobbling a little as I do. "I'll take the sofa." The magic I used to heal him has taken it out of me.

He grabs my hand and drags me back down. "No chance, there's enough room in the bed. Don't worry. I won't try anything." He shifts backward and lies down, eyes shutting instantly.

I feel myself getting tired, and my knees are shaking from the exertion of power I put into the spell to heal him. It was more power than I can spare, but for some reason, I'd risk my own life to save this man I hardly know.

I don't even bother getting out of my dress and flop down by his side. He's quick to roll over and mold himself to my back, wrapping a possessive arm around my waist. "Night, love," he murmurs, as his hot breath falls on my skin.

I bite my lip, feeling more turned on than should be physically possible right now. The exhaustion can't tame the fire burning inside of me. I shift my hips backward and press my ass hard into his crotch.

He groans, and I gasp as I feel how rock hard he is. "Don't tease me, Ilsa. I said I wouldn't try anything, but you are pushing your luck."

I swallow hard, wondering whether I want him to try anything or not. Conflict is all I've felt since he made me feel the way he did in that warm bay. Dragons and witches can't be together, and yet that thought threatens to tear my world apart.

His grip on my waist tightens as he pulls me against

his muscular chest. Heat floods my body at his touch, and the manly scent of him encasing me. It soothes me and eases all my anxiety.

It seems it's impossible to resist him. I've never heard of a mating bond between a dragon and a witch. Maybe it is having a similar effect on me as it has on him.

All my life, I've been in control. I don't like that it takes that away from me. There's no way for me to resist the man that makes me wild with need. His hard cock is settled between my ass cheeks, making me even needier.

Aiden kisses my neck softly. "How is it that I'm so desperate for you even while I'm in pain?" he whispers, moving his hand to my hip and squeezing gently. "Turn around, love."

I do as he says, knowing it would be impossible to resist him anything. His beautiful orange eyes are pure dragon now, flaring with pure desire. He captures my lips softly, searing them with a hot, passionate kiss.

I feel myself dampen between my thighs as the exhaustion melts away. Neither of us should have the energy to even kiss right now. Aiden groans against my lips. "Beautiful." He pulls away and stares at me, sending heat pulsing around every inch of my body.

I need him so badly as I claw onto his hard, muscular biceps. We went too far in that lake. I know we're about to cross the line again as I look into his eyes.

His hard cock pulses in my hand, dripping pre-cum all over the sheets.

My mouth waters at the thought of tasting him. "Isn't it my turn to taste you?" I ask.

He groans, and his eyes flick shut for a moment, before opening wide. "Fuck, yes." He shifts in the bed, so he's sitting on the edge.

I get out of bed and kneel in front of him.

His cock is rock hard and dripping cum all over the floor.

I moan as I take him into my hand and move it up and down his shaft slowly.

He laces his fingers in my hair, trying to pull my lips to the head of his cock.

I let him take control, feeling my arousal increase between my thighs. It doesn't make any sense. I hate not having control over everything, but I long to submit to him. His hard, muscular abs tense as his cock slips past my lips. A deep, guttural groan escapes him.

My tongue circles his thick, swollen head, teasing more pre-cum from him. It floods my tongue and fills my mouth with the masculine, salty taste of him. I moan around his cock, letting it sink to the back of my throat.

"That's it, love," He groans, tightening his grip on my hair. "Suck my cock."

I gag as he pushes my head down further on his cock. I can hardly breathe as I pull off him and stare up at him with wide eyes. "What the fuck?"

A handsome smirk twists onto his lips. "Sorry, love. Dragon shifters are naturally dominant." His brow furrows. "Don't you like it?" he asks, eyes moving to my hard, erect nipples.

I lick my bottom lip, knowing that I do like it. I've just never experienced a man treating me so roughly. I shrug. "I do, but—"

"But nothing, then." He yanks my hair again and pushes my mouth back onto him.

I open my lips willingly and let him sink back into my throat. It's almost impossible to breathe, and I gag, pulling back off him. "Fuck," I say.

He lets go of my hair. "I'll stop pushing you."

I feel disappointed that I can't take the size of him into the back of my throat. It's impossible. He's too large. I take his length back into my mouth, bobbing up and down as I try and fail to sink him further each time.

His shaft swells in my mouth, and he groans deeply. "Fuck, love. I'm going to come." Aiden's fingers twist in my hair to pull me off, but I keep sucking.

I let him sink into the back of my throat again, trying to make him come in my mouth. He roars above me as he explodes in my throat.

I swallow his cum as he pumps his cock in and out of my throat, draining his balls.

When he finally stops, he pulls himself out of my mouth. He bends down, and he kisses me hard and deep, tasting himself on my tongue. When he breaks away, we're both breathless. "Time to sleep, love." He kisses me softly before lifting me to my feet and guiding me back into bed.

We both settle down under the covers, and Aiden pulls me into his chest.

What are we doing?

We've just met, and now I'm wrapped in Aiden's embrace as if we're lovers. A witch should never trust a dragon, but I feel safe in his arms. My eyes flicker shut, and I fall to sleep quickly. Far more quickly than I should given the circumstances.

9

AIDEN

I wake in a room I don't recognize. My mind is hazy.

As I glance around, my gaze comes to a stop when I see her by my side. *Ilsa.* The moment I see her, all my memories come flooding back like a wave. Pain clenches around my heart as I remember Elaine's eyes as she slowly faded away in front of my eyes.

The men that killed my father came back for us. I got away, and Ilsa managed to patch me up in time, but Elaine is dead. Her mate and husband, Luke, won't know yet. He's the leader of the Nebraska pack, governed by Rhys, the wolf shifter king. Ever since he took control of New York, all the North American packs are under his rule.

If he thinks I had anything to do with her death, we'll have a war on our hands. I bring my hand to the area on my stomach where that bastard had stabbed me.

Ilsa's magic healed it so well, there's only a faint scar. It still hurts, though.

Ilsa stirs by my side, beautiful bright green eyes landing on me. "Are you okay?" she asks, sitting up and setting a hand on my shoulder.

I move my hand from my stomach. "Yes, it just hurts still."

She nods. "I may have healed the wound, but it will still hurt for a while." She shrugs. "Magic has it's perks, but there are often side-effects. It's not the same as healing naturally."

I smile at my mate. "Thanks for that, by the way. I think I was too exhausted last night to thank you properly." I feel my cock thicken as I remember what I did. "Other than shove my cock down your throat."

Her cheeks are bright red at the mention of her sucking my dick. "It's nothing." She shrugs as if it's no big deal, but I saw how she shook after helping me.

I raise a brow, but don't say anything else. My stomach aches as I move to the edge of the bed, resting my head in my hands. A heaviness settles on my chest as I remember Elaine's face, lifeless. I run a hand across the back of my neck, wondering if it's safe to go back to the castle or not.

"What's wrong?" Ilsa asks, setting a hand on my shoulder.

I shake my head. "I don't know what happened last night." My shoulders droop as I realize how badly I failed to protect my sister. It's embarrassing. I'm the king, and I couldn't protect her from them. "How will I know if the castle is safe or not?"

"You're not thinking of returning, are you?"

I turn around to face her. "Where else am I going to go?"

She shrugs. "Isn't it dangerous? The men who stormed the place might still be there."

I crack my neck, knowing she is right. Those men attempted a coup last night, trying to wipe my entire family out. Now I'm alone. My father's gone and my sister. I've got no one left in this world, except for the beautiful woman sitting next to me.

"I've got a cabin not too far from here." I meet Ilsa's gaze. "We can't risk staying here much longer."

She licks her bottom lip, drawing my attention to it. "We?" she asks.

I nod my head. "I told you, Ilsa. You are my mate. There's a threat to me out there, which means you are in danger too."

Conflict rages in her beautiful emerald eyes as she gazes into mine. "I'm not sure, Aiden."

"Please," I say, tucking a hair behind her ear. "I can't lose you too, love. I've lost all the family I've got."

Her eyes widen, and I realize I've just suggested she is like family to me. It's true. She's my mate.

First, my mother died and then my father, shortly followed by my sister.

Am I fated always to lose everyone close to me?

I won't lose her. I'll defy fate to ensure that doesn't

happen, but doubt creeps into my mind. Maybe I'm cursed.

"Okay, I'll come with you." Her brow furrows. "How long will we be there?"

"Hopefully not too long. I need time to figure out what to do."

I want to provide her stability, give her the answers, but I don't have them. In the space of a few days, I've gone from being a prince with no responsibilities to a king with the weight of the world on my shoulders.

All my life I've been preparing for this, but I never expected the time to come. At least, not so soon.

My father was young. If those men hadn't murdered him, he had many years of life left. It brings home the dangers of our life—a life I'm going to drag Ilsa into, like my father pulled her family into danger. I might not know what happened to them, but I'm sure the meeting with my father has something to do with it.

"Pack your bags, and we'll go right away."

She nods and grabs her bag, rushing around to collect her clothes and possessions. I watch her in awe. The beauty that has derailed my entire world and filled my life with rays of bright sunlight.

I've never felt more complete as I watch her. It feels like my life has only just started.

ILSA WALKS around the cabin with her arms wrapped

around herself. The sun is setting over the forest, and it casts an orange glow through the window, hitting her. It makes her look almost otherworldly. She looks like she was born to be here. Ilsa belongs in my private space—a place I've never bought anyone to before. A place I've spent more time than you would expect for a king.

I can imagine waking up next to her like I did this morning every morning for the rest of my life. It's an odd sensation but exciting.

"Do you like my little hideout?"

She glances at me and smiles. "Yeah, it's a bit different from the castle."

I nod. "That place can get stuffy." I pause a moment, scared she might think I'm being to forward. "I've never bought anyone here before."

Her brow raises. "No one?"

I shake my head, and her cheeks turn a dark pink. "You're the first."

She swallows hard and turns her attention back to the family photo hanging on my wall. "This is your family?" she asks.

Pain clutches at my heart. "Was my family. They're all dead."

She spins around. "Of course, sorry. I didn't mean to—"

"Don't worry, love. It's been a hard week. First, my father and then Elaine..." I shake my head, unable to find the words to explain how it makes me feel.

She steps toward me and sets a hand on my arm.

"You've lost a lot. It's okay not to be okay if that makes sense."

I nod my head. "It does." I rest my hand over hers and squeeze.

The moment our skin connects, that fire ignites. My sorrow is drowned out with pure need as I meet Ilsa's emerald gaze.

She swallows hard, her throat bobbing. "What now?" she asks, trying to diffuse the tension.

All it does is drive more tension between us. I need to claim her. That's what comes next. "You're mine, Ilsa." I pull her into my chest. "I need to be inside of you," I murmur, letting my lips tease against the sensitive skin at the base of her neck.

Her knees shake as she leans on me.

She's pure femininity. I run my hands down her perfect curves. I can't believe how perfect she is. There are no words that can define how beautiful the woman in my arms is.

Her plump lips part, and her tongue darts out over her bottom lip. "Then take me."

A part of my resolve snaps as my lips crash into hers. My cock is rock-hard and pulsing in my tight boxer briefs. It has been ever since I got this beauty into my cabin.

My tongue slips inside her mouth, kissing her deeply.

She moans against me, clawing onto my biceps. I love the way she wants to submit to me. Her tendency to give everything to me the moment she's in my arms feeds my dragon's desires.

When we part, she's flushed and breathless and so fucking perfect. "Strip," I order.

I don't have to ask her twice. She's quick to hook her fingers into the waistband of her pants and pull them down, before pulling off her t-shirt.

Once she's just in her underwear, she tilts her head to the side. "What about you?" she asks.

"What about me?" I narrow my eyes. "I'm in control here." I nod my head toward her. "Panties and bra off now," I growl.

A flash of defiance ignites in her eyes, and she folds her arms over her chest, covering her perfect, full breasts from my view. "Not until you take your clothes off."

I step toward her. "Are you defying me, Ilsa?"

I hear her heartbeat quicken at my tone, knowing she's excited about the prospect of me being dominant with her. I can tell by the heart rate but also by the way her breathing labors.

"Yes. Fair is fair," she says.

I shake my head. "I don't play fair, love." I grab her hand and pull her toward me, kissing her lips. Then, I spin her around and bend her over the arm of the sofa in my cabin.

"W-What are you doing?"

"I'm going to punish you for being a naughty girl."

She tenses, and I wonder if I'm pushing this too far.

Slowly, I caress her round ass cheek in my hand, before gently spanking the skin.

She cries out, but the pleasure laced in her voice is unmissable. "Aiden, what are you—"

I spank her other ass cheek, and she groans this time.

"Do you like me punishing you?" I ask, spanking both ass cheeks three more times.

She makes a satisfying whimpering sound that makes my cock so hard it hurts.

I let my hand slip down to the fabric of her panties, groaning at the wetness there. "You do like it. You are soaking wet."

"Fuck me," she moans.

The pressure in my pants builds as my cock strains to break free. "Oh, I will, but not yet." I spank her ass cheeks again. "I'm going to make you so needy that you beg me for my cock."

Her thighs visibly quiver at my words.

I move aside the thin fabric of her panties and kneel behind her. The scent of her arousal drives me wild and my mouth waters.

I feel my cock leaking into my boxer briefs but ignore it.

All I can do is focus on making her wild, as my breath teases against the dripping wet folds of her pretty pussy nestled between her thighs.

"Aiden, please," she moans.

I plunge my tongue into her sweet pussy, unable to

hold myself back any longer. She tastes like pure fucking sugar. I've never tasted anything as sweet as Ilsa.

I groan the moment I taste her. Somehow, she tastes better than I remember in that lake. She's pure femininity.

Ilsa gasps and bucks her hips backward, trying to drive my tongue deeper. I grab her hips and stop her from moving, digging my fingertips in hard. "Don't move," I growl, before licking her again.

The need to fuck her is driving me wild, but I want her to come and come until she's so desperate. I need her to want me as much as I need her.

I let my teeth brush against her clit gently, enticing a deep moan from her. "Oh, God, I'm going to come," she cries out as I replace my teeth with my fingers. I rub her to climax, licking her sweet juice spilling from her pussy.

This is only just beginning. By the time I finish with Ilsa, she won't remember her damn name. That's for sure.

10

ILSA

*I*t feels like my world explodes as my climax eases. Aiden doesn't let up. He's already working me into a frenzy again before it even ends. His fingers delve in and out of me without mercy.

"Aiden, please."

He spanks my ass cheek, sending a stinging pain through me. It lights up every nerve in my body. "I'm not done with you yet. "

I freeze as his tongue probes at my asshole. "What are you—"

He spanks my ass cheek again and continues to lick the tight ring of muscles.

I groan, wondering if he's broken me. It feels so dirty but amazing. His fingers curl deep inside of me. I feel every muscle in my body shake with need. Aiden has me so highly strung. I'm ready to explode.

No one has ever made me feel the same way as he

does. It's deep and powerful. I can't put into words the sensations he is sending through my body.

Our souls join somehow—it's spiritual and invigorating. I haven't felt this powerful since I was a child before the coven broke apart.

"Aiden," I gasp his name as he spanks my ass again before thrusting three fingers deep inside my pussy. His tongue still probes the sensitive nerves at my asshole. "Fuck. "

"That's it, love. I want you to come while I lick your pretty little asshole," he groans.

The dirty talk is all it takes to unravel me. I come apart, crying Aiden's name. Thank God this cabin is far away from any other homes, as I'm sure I'm so loud people would hear me a mile away.

"So sweet," he groans as his mouth leaves my ass, and I feel him standing.

I groan when I hear the sound of a belt buckle. I glance back at him, but he spanks my ass.

"Face forward."

I quiver in anticipation as his pants drop to the floor, followed by his boxer briefs and then his shirt.

Aiden grabs my hips and pulls me up, forcing me to stand. He presses my back into his naked form, letting me feel every dip and curve of his muscles. Not to mention, his thick cock pressing in between my butt cheeks. "Is this what you want?" he murmurs, biting my earlobe softly.

I groan. "Yes, please, Aiden. I need you."

He wraps his arms around me tightly, keeping my back against him. "Not sure you've come enough yet."

I whimper as a weakness spreads through my muscles. The thought of coming anymore makes me feel spent but needy. Aiden lifts me in his arms effortlessly and carries me into the back room of the cabin. There's a large bed in the center.

He sets me down and stares down at me, fisting his thick, swollen cock in his hands.

My mouth waters at the sight of him, erect and ready to take me. I let my fingers tease my aching nipples.

"That's it, baby, play with your pretty nipples for me." The heat in his eyes threatens to set me on fire. "I want you to make yourself come."

I bite my bottom lip. "Aren't you going to touch me?"

He shakes his head, smirking. "No, love. I want you to bring yourself to climax while you suck me." He steps forward and rests at the edge of the bed.

I eagerly crawl toward his cock, desperate to taste his cum again.

His cock twitches in front of my face as I reach for it, slowly tugging him with my hand.

He grabs my wrist hard and shakes his head. "I said suck it, baby, not touch it."

I let go of his shaft and open my mouth, letting my tongue dart out and taste the salty precum on the tip of his cock.

He forces his hips forward, and his cock slides into my throat immediately.

I gag on him, saliva spilling all over his shaft and balls.

He pulls back slightly, giving me a moment to compose myself, before thrusting back into my throat. His dominance is such a turn on.

Salty precum spills down my throat as I relax my gag reflex. All I focus on is breathing through my nose as Aiden starts to fuck my throat.

My fingers move over my clit as I suck on him, making him groan above me. It makes me feel powerful, making him feel as good as he has made me feel.

We're both set on making each other feel good, and I can't wait to feel him moving deep inside of me. He tightens his grip on my hair, as he starts to fuck my throat ruthlessly.

His eyes are pure dragon as he gazes down at me. He hardly looks human. I feel the tightness building deep inside of me still, as I rub my clit.

I'm going to come apart at any moment, and he knows it. The way he holds my gaze tells me that much. "That's it, Ilsa. I want you to come with my cock down your throat," he growls.

I feel his cock swell in my mouth.

"Fuck. I'm going to come, baby."

He thrusts once more and explodes, cum flooding my mouth and throat. I swallow every drop. His release coaxes mine as I come with my lips still around his shaft.

I pull off of him, moaning as I lick every drop of cum off him.

"Fuck, that was amazing," I breathe.

His eyes darken as he grabs my chin and kisses me hard and deep. When we break away, I'm breathless and needier.

I glance at his cock. He's still rock hard and ready for more. "Aiden, I need to feel you inside of me," I gasp, as he sucks on my hard, aching nipples.

He tilts my head back, pulling on my hair gently. "I'm going to give you what you need, baby." He pushes me back down on the bed and climbs over me. His muscles are tense.

I feel my body shake as his heavy cock settles against my clit. I've never felt so desperate to be joined to anyone before. He makes me insane with need. "Are you ready, love?"

I nod my head. "Never been more ready for anything."

He smiles as he moves his lips to mine. "Beg me, baby."

I bite my bottom lip. "Please fuck me, Aiden, right now."

He groans and lines his cock up with my dripping wet pussy.

I've never been this turned on before in my life. My nipples are hard peaks. My pussy is soaked.

Aiden holds my gaze as he thrusts deep inside of me.

My pussy stretches to his enormous size, as he slides inside. "Fuck. "

He bites my bottom lip gently, holding still inside of me. It gives me a moment to get used to his size deep inside of me. "So fucking tight," he groans.

I claw at his back with my fingertips, wanting to feel him move. "Fuck me now," I whisper.

There's a flash of fierce hunger in his eyes as he kisses me again, even harder this time. The desperation is on another level as we claw at each other. His fingers press into my hips possessively, making me moan.

He bites my bottom lip as he begins to move in and out of me. It feels like our souls merge the moment he begins to move—a deeply moving moment as we make love for the first time. Aiden's eyes hold such powerful emotion as we maintain eye contact.

I dig my fingertips into his biceps as he moves over me.

My eyes roll back in my head as he sinks in harder and deeper with each thrust. The need between us increasing.

He stops with a mischievous glint in his eyes.

"Don't stop," I moan.

"Tell me how much you want it, Ilsa," he groans, keeping his lips against mine.

I'm shaking so much I can hardly speak. "I want it more than anything, Aiden."

He growls a deep sound before gripping hold of my

hips again. He pounds into me hard and fast. I gasp at the size of him stretching me.

His pupils narrow and elongate more than I've ever seen. I bite my bottom lip as he growls above me. His teeth are sharper now and pointed.

He leans down and sinks them softly into my collarbone. It's a wonder he doesn't pierce the skin, but the pain is electric.

"Aiden," I moan his name, feeling the pleasure build deep inside of me.

I claw my fingernails into his back, and he nips at my lip in a warning.

"No clawing." He grips hold of my hips hard, and then flips me over effortlessly. He hardly offers me a second to get used to the new position as he slips back inside.

I arch my back, loving how much he fills me.

He spanks my ass, making me gasp. "Fuck, you are so perfect," he groans, gripping my hips even harder as he roughly takes me. He's hard and unforgiving, and I love it.

I feel the fluttering ignite deep within me, and I know he feels it too.

"That's it, love. I want to feel you come with my cock deep inside of you," he growls, picking up the pace even more.

"Fuck," I moan, as stars filter into my vision. The sensation is so intense, so consuming. It feels like I'm floating above my body as my climax crashes through me. My body trembles, my knees can no longer hold me up as I collapse flat onto the bed.

Aiden roars behind me as he pumps two last times and then explodes. My breathing is erratic as I remain face down. His weight rests on me, grounding me.

Finally, he frees me and flops down by my side. I shift onto my back, and he pulls me into him.

I rest my hand on his chest and glance up at him. The thought of speaking right now scares me. I don't want to ruin the moment we shared. It was special, magical. I've never felt like this around another person before.

He kisses the top of my head. "I didn't hurt you, did I?" he asks.

I shake my head. "No, definitely not. The opposite."

"Good, I never want to hurt you, Ilsa." He presses his lips to mine and kisses me deeply, increasing the desire for him already.

I'm sure we won't be doing much else this evening. Something tells me we won't be able to drag ourselves out of this bed.

THE BIRDS SING in the trees as the sun slowly creeps over the dense cover of the forest. Aiden's little cabin in the woods is quaint. I step outside of the front door and take a deep breath, enjoying the fresh, forest air.

He's still asleep, and I don't blame him. We hardly

slept last night. I wrap my shawl more tightly around my arms as the wind picks up.

My family might be out there somewhere, and I'm desperate to find them. Guilt floods me as I've been thrown off track yesterday, spending it here. Aiden consumed all of my attention, taking it away from what matters most—saving them.

I walk in the direction of flowing water. This place is more beautiful than my home in San Francisco. All my life, I've lived in a city and away from the true beauty of nature. A life with Aiden could give me everything I've longed for—freedom.

I wander away from the cabin, following the running water. Last night was the best night of my life. When I set out to find my family, Aiden was the last thing I expected to find. I've still got reservations. His father invited my brother here.

How can they disappear?

Something about King Kendall's insistence of meeting with my brother felt off to me when he told me about it. My parents agreed to take him, eager to see if the king could help us.

I should have gone with them, but they insisted someone needed to stay home. Unfortunately, that someone was me because I didn't even believe it would achieve anything to meet with the king.

All I want to do is believe in Aiden. Perhaps it's the instincts related to the mating bond, but all I feel is uncertainty. I shake my head as I reach the edge of a small stream, no wider than a meter across.

The fish swim beneath the rushing water. Nature should always be part of a witch's life, but we've lost our connection to the earth as the world modernizes at a rapid rate. I can't imagine anything better than living out here with Aiden. I shake my head. Even if he's my mate, this can never work— we can't be together.

"Ilsa," Aiden shouts my name, his voice full of panic.

"Over here, Aiden," I call back.

He rushes down the hill toward the stream, and the tension eases from his shoulders the moment he sees me. "You scared me half to death." He walks over to me and takes my hand. "Don't wander off without me, do you understand?"

I shake my head and pull my hand from his. "I'll go for a walk if I want to." I cross my arms over my chest. "I can take care of myself, Aiden."

He sighs heavily and runs a hand through his hair. "I know." He turns away and wanders down the stream, his shoulders tense.

I follow after him. "What is bothering you?"

He shakes his head. "Everyone I love dies. What if I'm cursed?"

Love.

It seems a bit early to bring up love, considering I met the guy two days ago.

I reach out to him. "Aiden, you're not cursed."

He turns around, and his eyes are brimming with unshed tears. "You don't know that. First, it was my mother, then my father, and now Elaine…" He trails off, and his concern is unspoken. "I can't lose you too."

I shake my head. "You won't." I pull him into an embrace, feeling oddly vulnerable.

How can he be scared of losing me when we only met the day before yesterday? It makes no sense.

Somehow, I feel the same. The thought of not being with Aiden threatens to tear me apart. He's become a part of me so quickly.

11

AIDEN

A fae male stands in front of me. His bright blue eyes glow in the dim light of the forest. "You are exactly who I've been searching for."

My heart pounds, wondering if this guy poses a threat. Ilsa is only a ten meters away by the stream, searching for fire wood. "Do I know you?"

He shakes his head. "We've not met, but you'll know me by reputation. Flynn, king of the fae." He bows slightly.

I grit my teeth, knowing that this was going to come eventually. Relief filters through me as I know instantly neither me nor Ilsa are in danger from this man. The one thing I didn't expect was for the faerie king to show up in the middle of nowhere like this. "Have you been following me?"

A mischievous smirk flits onto his lips. "Perhaps. I have an essential proposition for you."

"Like you had for my father?" I ask.

He nods. "Yes, but I know you will hear me out. You are different from your father."

He's got that right. I've never had the same hatred he has for inter-species romance or integration. When Elaine mated to that wolf, it broke his heart. I still saw the same Elaine, but for him, she had become tainted.

He tried every way he could to break them apart, and I stood by and did nothing. It was brutal and selfish, and if I could go back and do it all over again, I would.

"Yes, I'm different from him, but what you want to do is insane."

He laughs. "No. It's the most sensible proposition anyone has had on this planet for millennia." He steps forward, making me tense.

Dragons and fae aren't renowned for getting along, although we don't butt heads with them as severely as our wolf counterparts. "Why segregate everyone? Humans, Dragons, wolves, faeries, and even witches." There's a sparkle in his eyes as he says the last one, and I wonder if he knows about Ilsa. The fae can learn things many would dream impossible. "Oh, and don't forget the vampires."

My eyes widen at that. "Impossible. They can't live side by side in harmony with humans. It's like asking lions to live with lambs and not harm them." I shake my head. "In answer to your question, because it's what has always been done even before the truth became known."

He tilts his head to the side. "Does that mean it is

what should be done?" He flicks a coin into the air, catching it. "I've seen firsthand the power in joining with other species. I'm confident in time you will too."

I know he has, and I've got a feeling I have too. Ilsa is my mate. The woman I'm destined to be with for the rest of my life. He doesn't have to convince me, but I'm not ready to speak it out loud. Most dragon shifters wouldn't like the idea. Change is difficult for most when it's on the kind of scale Flynn is suggesting.

"Why are you here, Flynn?" I ask, folding my arms over my chest.

He runs a hand through his dark black hair. "I'm here to invite you to a meeting."

I thought this was coming. Flynn invited my father to dine with him at his home countless times, and every time my father declined. I'm pretty sure he believed Flynn would try to murder him once he was there.

"What kind of meeting?"

He closes the gap between us further and holds out an invitation card.

I don't take it but read it from afar.

Flynn invites you to attend the first council meeting.

Tomorrow

Ten in the morning sharp at the old council chambers of the fae.

"What council?" I ask, glancing up and searching the mischievous eyes of the fae king.

What is he playing at?

He clears his throat. "I intend to create a council to

help start the integration of our kinds into one society. Rhys Verne has already accepted, and Vladimir, it is just you left." He tilts his head to the side. "You don't want the dragon shifters to be un-represented, do you?"

I shake my head, a little stunned that he managed to get Rhys Verne to agree. There was a time when he hated fae. "What about witches and warlocks?" I ask.

Flynn passes the invitation back into my hands. "What about them?"

I shrug. "Who will represent them at the meeting?"

A knowing smirk twists onto his lips. "I don't know any witches or the way their hierarchy works, but if you know a worthy subject, by all means, bring her along."

I narrow my eyes at him. There's no doubt that he knows about Ilsa. The question is, how does he know?

If he has been following us, then it would make sense. The fae have unmatched senses when it comes to detecting species of any person they happen across. He would know that Ilsa was a witch. My heart pounds unevenly as I sense her moving away from the stream, toward us.

Flynn's brow raises as he notices the tension in my shoulders. "What do you say?"

I glance down at the invitation, staring at it for a moment. "Have you heard about the attack at the castle?"

He nods. "Yes, I'm sure I can help you with that. The people who attacked you are the kind of people I'm set out to stop."

I sigh heavily, before nodding. "Okay, I'll be there."

He smiles widely, bearing his sharp canines. "Perfect. See you tomorrow." He winks, before vanishing in a haze of blue light.

Ilsa has been lingering to my left, but once she sees him leave, I sense her move again. "What the hell was that?" she asks.

I hold out the invitation. "The fae king."

Her eyes widen as she takes the invitation out of my hand. "Are you going to go?" she asks after a quick skim over the words. My father always refused to meet Flynn or discuss his plans. I need to do something different, as my father was too traditional in his ways and ideas.

"Yes, I agreed."

She sighs. "What if it's a trap?"

I shake my head. "Flynn has been trying to get my father to agree to a meeting for years. He's a peaceful king."

Ilsa doesn't look convinced as she turns toward the cabin. "We should get back. I feel exposed out here."

Whoever has taken over the castle could find us here too. I was at ease here, but Flynn's appearance makes me doubt our safety.

Ilsa squeezes my hand. "What are you thinking?"

I shake my head. "I'm not sure how safe it is here now."

She smiles. "Fae magic can shock. If it was shifters that were after you back at the castle, you have nothing to worry about."

"How can you be so sure?"

She shrugs. "I'm a witch. Magic is part of me."

It makes sense, but dragon shifters aren't powerless. "All dragon shifters have witches on their side."

She shakes her head as she reaches for the door to the cabin. "They don't have the power the fae do."

I let her go first and then check our surroundings, searching for any sign of movement. It's about ten minutes until dark closes in, and the temperature will drop. I need to get the fire going before that happens.

Dragon shifters can survive in the cold, but not witches.

I follow into the cabin, shutting the door behind me. I pull the bolts across, before securing the wooden drawbar.

When I turn back around, Ilsa is watching me curiously. "Are you okay?"

"Yes, I just want tomorrow to come quickly. We need Flynn's help to find your family and find out who has taken over my home."

She steps toward me and takes my hand, leading me toward the sofa in the living room. "Keep your mind off that for now. There's nothing we can do tonight."

I glance down at our entwined hands. "You're right. I want to learn more about my mate."

Her cheeks darken a deep red at that. "What do you want to know?"

"What's your favorite food?"

She smiles. "Pizza. Always pizza. What about you?"

"I'm a dragon, so it's got to be steak." I hold my hands up. "Meat eater through and through."

She nods. "I love steak too."

I raise a brow. "Really, a lot of the witches I know are vegetarians."

Ilsa shakes her head. "Not me or my family. Although, I doubt we eat as much meat as dragons."

I laugh at that. "I doubt it. We can eat a lot." I glance over at the kitchen. "Speaking of which, I'm starving right now."

Her stomach rumbles in response. "Me too."

"I'm pretty certain that I've got some homemade pizza in the freezer."

"Homemade? Are you a cook?" she asks, teasingly.

I shake my head. "No, but I like to cook when I'm alone here. At the castle, people do everything for me. This is my escape." I open the freezer and fish out the pizza I made before, stepping toward the oven and turning it on.

I press my hand against the glass and focus my heat into it, speeding it up. Then, I place the pizza slices on the tray and put it in.

Ilsa sits at the old oak table in the center of the kitchen.

I grab a bottle of red wine and hold it up. "How about a glass of Cabernet Sauvignon?"

Her eyes light up. "Hell, yes. I need a drink."

I pour us each a glass and then sit at the table next to her. "Cheers, love." I clink my glass against hers.

She smiles, but it's half-hearted. "Cheers."

"What's wrong?"

She shrugs. "I miss my family."

I take her free hand in mine. "I know, but we will find them, I promise."

She sighs heavily. "You can't be certain of that but thank you." She smiles. "They would love you."

I squeeze her hand. "Even though I'm a dragon shifter?"

She smiles. "Of course. They don't care about that sort of thing and never have."

It's a relief to hear that. I can't deal with conflict from Ilsa's family over our bond. It's bad enough that the rest of my kind will likely revolt against the pairing.

I look at our hands entwined. "I wish I could introduce you to mine, but unfortunately, they're all gone." I sigh heavily, feeling the weight of my loss crushing me. It's worse because I can't even take the time to grieve properly. Elaine's body has probably been dumped somewhere, she's not been put to rest properly.

"I couldn't say my father would have been thrilled, but had my mother been alive, she was very different. Elaine, too, she was…" I feel my throat close up a bit with emotion, unable to keep speaking.

Ilsa squeezes my hand. "I'm so sorry, Aiden."

I nod and clear my throat. "I'd better check on the pizza." I've always had difficulty expressing my emotions. I guess it's because it was discouraged by my father. "It's ready," I say, grabbing the oven mitts and getting the pizza out.

She walks over and gathers two plates. "Mmm, pepperoni is my favorite."

I smile. "Mine too."

We share a glance, but every time our eyes meet, my mind goes to one thing. I break the eye contact and dish up the pizza, before joining her back at the table.

"I hope you like it, as I said, I'm not a chef."

She takes a bite, and her eyes widen. "It's delicious. I wish I could make pizza this good without magic." A mischievous spark enters her eyes.

"Are you telling me we waited for that to cook, and you could have conjured us one instantly?"

She smiles. "Maybe, but I wanted to taste your homemade pizza."

I laugh and tuck into the food. I feel guilty that with Ilsa, my grief seems to fade into the background. The loss of Elaine and my father hurt, but somehow, my mate's presence makes it easier. I find it hard to sink into despair with her around.

ILSA

*M*y heart pounds unevenly in my chest as I stand outside of the council chambers. Aiden insisted I should attend this meeting, but as a witch, I feel exposed and vulnerable. Out of all the species gathering here today, the witches were the most repressed. Only a few hundred years ago, they were hunted by fae, dragons, and wolves, along with hung by humans.

All of them attacked us, all of them except for vampires. We ended up often having a slightly uneasy alliance with them. Aiden insists this might help us find my family or begin to find answers as to where they are.

Flynn is a powerful fae king. If anyone can help locate them, it's him. I take in a deep breath, knowing it's about time. Aiden and I didn't go in together to ensure we don't arouse suspicion. No one knows publicly about our mating bond. I'm not sure we can ever really be together.

My family would be shocked if they learned the truth. The way I've been acting with Aiden, shacked up in a motel with him. I shake my head and wrap my fist against the solid oak door of the council chambers the guards led me to.

A knock at the door sounds, and he stops speaking.

"Come in," a voice calls.

I twist the doorknob and step inside, trying to fill every step with confidence. All eyes are on me, but the only eyes I can feel burning into me are Aiden's.

"I feel you are missing someone out, your majesty." I bow my head, showing respect to the king of the fae. "I don't see representation here for witches." My eyes meet Aiden's, and I can't help the heat that pulses through me. Anytime we're near, it's like a magnet is pulling all my attention to him.

Flynn nods his head, a small, knowing smile on his lips. "Of course, miss?" His eyes flick between Aiden and me.

"Ilsa," I say.

He smiles. "Ilsa, take a seat."

I swallow hard as I realize the only free seat is by Aiden's side. Somehow, I've got to make it seem like we've never met, even though we've been inseparable since the night we met.

Flynn claps his hands. "We have all species here that I am aware of. Rhys will speak for the shifters of North

America and across the globe, as will Aiden." He glances at a muscular, tattooed man with pale skin. "Vlad is the king of the vampires, and such our alliance is with you, be it an uneasy one."

My stomach churns as he grins, bearing his fangs. "I'm not sure what you are worried about, faerie, scared I might get a taste for faerie blood?"

Flynn shakes his head and moves on. "Now, I invite Ilsa to speak for the witches in our council. To align our people and allow integration between all our kinds."

She bows her head, smiling.

"Lastly, Lucy and Anastasia will represent humans. They have as much a right as any human in my eyes."

I notice Vlad shifts uncomfortably in his chair—eyes darken with what looks like irritation. If I didn't know any better, I'd say he can think of a human better suited to the role. However, he doesn't speak out.

The vampire's eyes are dark and soulless—almost black. Aiden's knee brushes against mine in an attempt to stop me from staring, all it does is drive me wild. I set my hand on his knee and squeeze gently, making him groan softly.

"Does anyone have any questions about the alliance we are forming here today?" Flynn asks, glancing directly at Rhys. If I were to wager anything, those two must have the most friction. Wolves and faeries have fought for millennia.

"No, mate," Vlad says in a British accent. "Just get on with this bullshit. I'm fucking starving, and you've got two juicy humans on offer right here." He licks his lips as he moves his attention between Lucy and Anastasia. Typical vampires. They have no control over their urges or their appetites.

Rhys growls at the vampire. It's a risk. Uniting creatures like this in one room isn't easy. I admire Flynn for what he is doing, but all I can think of is finding out the truth. The truth about what happened to my family.

Vlad holds up his hand. "Don't bite my fucking head off. What do you expect when you trap a hungry vampire in a room with two humans for too long?"

"Enough," Flynn calls, clapping his hands. "Fine, you can be the first to sign your contract and swear your loyalty to this council." Flynn passes him a piece of paper and an old-fashioned quill.

He takes it, reading through the contract before him. "Fine, where's the ink?"

Flynn smirks and hands him a knife. "You must write it in your blood."

He shakes his head. "Slight problem, I'm undead. How the fuck do you expect me to bleed for this?"

I stand, knowing that I can use magic to get around that issue. "I can help with that," I say, waving my hands toward him. Red magic shoots from my fingertips into the vampire. "Cut your wrist now as it will only last so long."

Vlad cuts his wrist without a moment's hesitation. The blood pours into the ink well, and his gaze meets mine for the first time. There's a spark of admiration there. "Nice trick, Ilsa." He dips the quill into the blood and signs his name, pushing it away. "I'm out of here." He slams down the quill, standing. "See you all at the next bullshit meeting." He disappears in a heartbeat, moving at vampire speed. There's one thing I'll give vampires. They are fucking fast.

Flynn is next to sign his name before he passes it to Aiden. He doesn't read the document, but he doesn't need to. I have already read it from afar, using my magic to listen in on Vladimir's thoughts. It's ironclad. Not to mention, I trust Flynn. I may not know him, but I believe we can trust him by reputation.

He essentially has witches for children. They are half-fae, but half-human. Aiden squeezes my knee under the table and gives me a quick wink as he passes the document into my hand. I glance down at it and then take the knife, cutting enough to spill blood into the magically cleaned ink well.

Fae are powerfully skilled at magic in different ways to witches. I sign my name in blood before sliding it along to Rhys. The wolf shifter and his mate are the last to sign.

Anastasia's belly is big and round with their fourth child. I can't deny that the world we live in is changing drastically.

Would it be so insane for a dragon and a witch to be together?

I know the answer is yes, even as we sit at a council meeting designed to change everything. Witches and dragons have never mixed, whereas there have always been romances between shifters and humans.

Aiden laughs, breaking me out of the daze I'd fallen into. "I'm not sure how you get away with being so scared of blood, considering your mate is a wolf shifter." He's talking to Anastasia, as Rhys cuts her hand and squeezes the blood into the vial.

"There, ready to sign." He passes the quill into her hand.

I watch her as she signs, before setting down the contract and putting her hands on the bump at her stomach—a boy. I'm one-hundred percent certain. A fact I'm sure Rhys would be delighted to learn.

"Thank you, Anastasia. It looks like the contract is complete." Flynn clears his throat. "I look forward to working with all of you to make this world a better place." He claps his hands. "Council meeting adjourned."

My eyes remain fixed on the happy couple, as Rhys helps her to her feet.

"Anastasia," I say the girl's name before I can reconsider. "Would you like to know the sex of your baby?"

She glances at Rhys, who shrugs. "Sure, why not," she says, flicking her long strands of red hair over her shoulders.

I smile, glancing right at Rhys. "Congratulations, your prince is almost here."

He smiles. "Seriously?"

I nod in response.

Rhys grabs her and kisses her softly. It makes my heart ache to see them together like that. Will there be a time when Aiden and I can be so open together?

"At last, a boy to tip the scales," he says.

I turn my attention away from them and set my sights on Aiden. Flynn is talking with him in hushed tones, glancing over at me.

I leave the happy couple and approach.

Flynn smiles and nods at me, stopping their conversation instantly. "I'm glad Aiden took the hint and invited you today." His eyes flash with playfulness. "I also believe I may be able to help with locating your family. Although you will have to leave it with me."

He glances over at Rhys and Anastasia. "If you excuse me, I've got something I must do. We'll talk tonight over dinner." He gives me a nod before rushing away.

My brow furrows as I glance at Aiden. "Dinner?"

He nods. "Yes, he thinks he can help you find your family, Ilsa." His hands move to my hips almost on instinct, and he draws me close.

"How does he know about us?" I ask, tilting my head slightly. "I thought we agreed not to tell anyone."

He shrugs. "I didn't tell him. The guy is psychic or something."

That doesn't sound right. Fae are powerful but not psychic. I have heard that they have a fantastic sense of awareness and smell. My cheeks heat as I wonder if he could smell me on Aiden that day in the forest. It wouldn't surprise me.

I had kept a reasonable distance after detecting him, unaware it was the fae king. Most fae have accepted the radical change he has set out to enforce, but countless still oppose him. Fae can be cruel and brutal if they don't like you, and many of them don't like witches.

"I feel a bit uneasy about it."

Aiden shakes his head. "Flynn can be trusted. Look what he's doing to unite all of us." He wraps an arm around my shoulders and pulls me close.

I breathe in his scent, letting it encase me. I've never felt more protected than I do wrapped in his arms. I just hope that Flynn can help us find my family and give Aiden a way to take back his castle from the people that killed his sister and father.

AIDEN

I squeeze Ilsa's hand as we stand in front of the grand, looming oak doors to Flynn's castle. She's uncertain about this, but I'm not. Flynn isn't the kind of person who would double-cross us. It doesn't help him in any way.

I understand her concern, though. Witches and Fae have never mixed in the past. The fae have a lot of natural enemies in this world, so it's ironic their king wants to bring everyone together.

I wrap on the door and keep my hand firmly laced with Ilsa's. She tries to pull away as the door swings open, but I keep hold of her. I'm fed up with her trying to hide what this is. She's my mate—my world. I want everyone to know that.

A tall, skinny fae male opens the door. "Come in."

Ilsa glances at me nervously as I pull her through the door into the grand castle. It's similar in size to mine but light and airy in comparison. I'd expect nothing less from a faerie.

"Follow me," the servant who let us in says.

I squeeze Ilsa's hand, trying to instill confidence in her. She is uneasy around all beings, but particularly fae for some reason. I saw how she spoke to Rhys without much trouble, but witches and wolves have never really clashed.

We walk down a long corridor lined with paintings until the man comes to a stop outside of a room. He raps the door three times.

"Come in," Flynn calls from the other side.

The man opens the door and steps inside, with us just behind him. "Your guests have arrived, sir."

He nods his head. "Thank you."

Lucy, Flynn's wife, is sitting by his side. I'm thankful that she is here, as she may help ease Ilsa's anxiety. It's setting me on edge too.

Flynn stands and walks over to me, patting me on the shoulder. "So glad you could make it." He smiles at Ilsa. "I'm looking forward to getting to know my two newest council members better."

Ilsa doesn't say anything only stares at him warily.

"We are looking forward to that too," I say, squeezing Ilsa's hand.

He smiles. "Come on, let's eat. I hope you don't mind vegetarian food." Flynn gives me a sheepish look. "I know it's not exactly a dragon's natural food, but meat isn't prepared in this household."

I bow my head, but my stomach disagrees with him. "Of course, we're happy to eat whatever you do."

"Ilsa, why don't you sit by Lucy's side?" Flynn suggests.

She looks at me uncertainly, before nodding her head. "Of course."

Flynn smiles. "Ilsa, you have nothing to fear from us." He tilts his head to the side. "I know the witches and the fae haven't got on in the past, but everything is changing now. I promise."

Some of the tension visibly eases from her shoulders as she smiles and takes a seat by Lucy.

"Help yourself," Flynn says, signaling toward the food laid out on the table.

I grab a spoon and pile a load of salad onto my plate, trying to be polite. Dragons mainly eat meat, but I can stomach it for now.

"I'm sorry it's not your normal meal, Aiden." He shrugs. "The fae aren't meat-eaters."

I nod. "Not to worry. I'm well aware of the fae's diet." I break off some bread and set it on the plate.

Ilsa hasn't yet touched anything as Lucy speaks to her. Flynn clears his throat. "You have questions for me about two subject, don't you?"

I raise a brow, surprised he's so quick to jump into that. "Yes, I want to know if the people who killed my sister are still at the castle."

Flynn's expression turns serious. "Yes, they are, but I will happily help you reclaim it with my men."

My brow furrows. "What's the catch?"

"There is no catch. You're not exactly going to be much use on the council if you have been dethroned, are you?"

He has a point, although they can't dethrone me like that. "Is someone suggesting they are the new monarch?"

Flynn nods, and there's hesitation on his face. "Yes. I thought you might have heard by now."

I shake my head. "Who is it?"

"Charles Anderson."

Numbness spreads through every inch of my body the moment he says that name. Charles has been my best friend since we were children.

Would he betray me like this?

"Are you sure?" I ask, my voice is hoarse.

He nods. "Certain. He has claimed responsibility for both your father's and sister's death." He swallows hard. "He has a bounty on your head too."

I clench my fists by my side. A mix of hurt, rage, and pure shock mingles inside of me as I try to process this information. Charles has betrayed me. He was the only other person, besides Ilsa, who I gave a damn about in this world. Charles is the reason I've got no family. He's the reason that the only family I have left is Ilsa.

Flynn pats my shoulder softly. "I'm sorry, Aiden. I know you two were close."

I nod and grab my glass of wine, downing it in one. "Don't worry. I will bring Charles down."

He smirks. "Dragons are strong, but they're not the best fighters. My men will help you." His attention moves to Ilsa. "As for your mate's family, I know where they are, but it might not be easy to get them out."

I narrow my eyes. "Are you saying they are alive?"

He lifts his glass of wine to his lips and takes a sip. "For now, yes, but not for long."

Panic races through me, and a question I dread rests on the tip of my tongue. Before I can ask it, Flynn speaks, "Yes, your father was involved. He was more brutal than you could ever know."

"In what sense?" I ask.

He rubs a hand across the back of his neck. "I'm not sure I'm the right person to reveal this information to you."

"Who is then?" I shrug. "There's no one left to tell me. All of my family are dead."

"Good point." He sighs heavily. "Your father has run a prison camp for a long while. They are hidden in the mountains and protected by ancient enchantments. I know, because my father set them for him when I was young. They are supernatural concentration camps. Your father has been the one diminishing witches and warlocks population for years." He pauses for a moment. "There may be quite a few surprises there, but that's all I'm going to say about the matter."

It feels like my world starts to spin.

Is it possible that my father could be that cruel?

As I think about that question, I realize the answer is

a resounding yes. My father was cruel to Elaine. He threatened to tear her and her mate part if he ever saw them again. It means he is capable of much worse when it comes to people outside of our family.

I swallow a lump of bread I'd been chewing. "Are you saying that even now he's gone, the camps continue to operate?"

He nods. "The camps continue to run until there is no one left alive. I'm sure the shifters that work there will wonder why there hasn't been any new offerings, but they are shut off entirely from the outside world by the enchantment."

"You are certain Ilsa's parents, and brother are there?"

Flynn nods. "Of course, it's the place your father takes all witches and warlocks lured to a meeting." He stares sadly at the glass of wine in his hand. "I tried everything I could to get your father to see reason, but all the while, he would laugh at my attempts to integrate all species on this planet." He meets my gaze. "He often called me weak, but I didn't take it to heart." He pauses a moment. "No offense meant, but he was the weak one."

I shake my head. "None taken. I can't believe I've been so blind all this time." I narrow my eyes. "Why did Charles kill my father? Was it for power, or another reason?"

Flynn stares at me with uncertainty flaring in his bright blue eyes. He opens his mouth to answer, but

Lucy clears her throat. "What are you two talking about?" she asks.

"We are talking about the coup at Aiden's castle, princess. Why?"

She shakes her head. "I thought this meal was to get to know each other better. I, for one, want to hear all about how Aiden and Ilsa met." She shrugs. "You both were very discreet at the meeting for fated mates."

Ilsa turns bright red at that.

"Do you want to tell them the story, love?"

She shakes her head. "No, I'll leave that to you."

I smile, finding it adorable how embarrassed she is about that night. There's nothing embarrassing about the way we met. "We met the same night they took over the castle at the ball Lance held." I pause a moment. "Did Lance have anything to do with the takeover?" I ask, glancing at Flynn.

He shrugs. "I'm not sure. I haven't heard anything about him."

A sinking feeling settles in my gut as I remember what an asshole I was to him when we last spoke. He could be dead for all I know. I can't believe how blind I was to my best friend's scheming.

"Enough of that. You are telling us how you met." Lucy claps her hands together, breaking me out of the daze I'd fallen into.

"Of course, Ilsa came into the ball with the intention of learning where her family was. The moment she stepped into the ballroom, I knew she was my mate."

Lucy smiles at Flynn. "Sounds familiar, although Flynn broke into my home."

Ilsa gasps. "Didn't you freak out?"

Lucy shakes her head. "I was so powerfully attracted to him. I could hardly think straight."

Ilsa's pink cheeks darken to red, and she looks at her plate.

"We danced before I stole her away and told her she was my mate." I glance at Ilsa. "She wasn't so powerfully attracted to me since she ran away." I run a hand through my hair. "I ended up chasing her out of the castle."

Lucy smiles. "And, then what?"

"I took her on a flight to Lake Tahoe, and we swam. Then we parted ways." I feel sadness grip at my chest as I remember what came next. "I watched Ilsa drive away and then entered my castle to my sister's screams." I glance down at the table. "You know the rest."

Lucy nods. "Yes, I'm very sorry to hear about your sister, Aiden." She sighs. "It sounds like it was the perfect night until then."

She's right. It was perfect until that point. Charles destroyed everything, and I won't rest until I kill him. The betrayal hurts me more than I can put into words, but that pain feeds the rage inside me. The next time I see him, I will tear him apart, if it's the last thing I do.

Flynn shifts in his seat. "You'll need that rage if you are going to bring about change." He nods. "And, if you are going to save your mate's family from the mountain prison."

Ilsa gives me a questioning look, as she didn't hear our conversation earlier. "You know where they are?"

"I'm ninety-nine percent sure, yes." Flynn nods. "Aiden's father created a prison for the supernatural, and if your brother was invited to meet with him, that's where they will be."

I realize that this looks bad on me. Ilsa doesn't understand that I didn't know. As our gazes meet, it's impossible to ignore the flash of hurt in her eyes. It cuts me more than she'll ever know. The fact she thinks I'd ever lie to her or keep something like this from her hurts.

I can't lie to her, she's my mate. Our bond is tenuous on her side, and I need to navigate this carefully. I need to prove to her that I'd never do anything to hurt her.

I L S A

*C*an *I truly trust Aiden?*

He may be my mate, but how could he be unaware of a prison camp for witches operating not far from his own home. His father set it up for fuck's sake.

Ever since we found out, I'm torn. I'm unsure whether or not to accept Aiden's help to break them out or to go it alone.

His father has killed countless numbers of my kind. I know that doesn't define who he is, but I can't shake the feeling that we aren't meant for each other.

I feel my chest ache as that thought enters my mind. I've given all of myself to Aiden in a way I've never done before with anyone. Not just my body, but my heart and soul too. I've jumped in fully and accepted the way I feel.

What if I made a mistake?

Aiden appears in the door behind me, making me

jump. "Morning, love." He looks uncertain as he runs a hand through his hair slowly. "Are we going to talk?"

"About what?" I ask, turning my attention back to the mirror in front of me.

He swallows. "About the fact you don't believe you can trust me after what you learned last night?"

How the fuck does he know that?

"I never said—"

"You don't have to. It was written all over your face at dinner. Then, when we got back, you weren't exactly hands-on like you have been."

I feel my cheeks heat. "Maybe I was just tired." I shrug.

He moves into the bathroom, approaching me. "Ilsa, you can't lie to me. I'm your mate. My senses are second to none when it comes to you."

I'm in so deep. I can feel my distrust eroding from Aiden's intense stare. "Okay, it's hard to accept that your father has some torture camp for witches in the mountains close to your home, and you had no idea about it."

A flash of hurt flits onto his face. "You have to believe me, love. My father always believed I was weak." His Adam's apple bobs as he swallows. "That's why he kept this from me because I wouldn't have stood by it."

It makes sense, but I've always had trouble trusting. It's even harder when it comes to dragon shifters or faeries. They've oppressed witches for too long. Now, two of them are asking me to trust them. "I find it hard to trust, Aiden. I hardly know you."

He nods. "I understand but let me prove myself to you."

I bite my bottom lip. "Why are you so desperate for this to work?"

"Because I'm yours, and you are mine."

That statement is so simple and yet so complicated. I can't be Aiden's, and Aiden can't be mine. "It can't work." I shake my head. "You're the king of the dragon shifters."

He smiles at me in the mirror. "Yes, I am, and I'm also your mate."

In a blink of an eye, everything has changed. My family disappeared, and now I'm falling for a dragon shifter against my will. There's nothing I can do about it. He's right. We fit together. We're made for each other, even if it doesn't work in the real world. "Witches and dragons aren't supposed to be together."

He wraps his strong arms around me. "Well, we'll have to break the mold, won't we?"

I know changing years of tradition isn't that easy. Brutality is a part of shifter nature, and a lot of that brutality was directed at witches and warlocks for centuries, if not millennia. Our power was feared, even though we're weaker than the fae. "I don't think it's that easy."

"When my mother was alive, she loved my father." Aiden's eyes glisten with tears. "She told me all the time that true love is the most powerful magic on the earth." He meets my gaze. "I've believed that ever since. She was an amazing woman, and unfortunately, her death led to my father's brutal nature." He grimaces. "Had she been alive, I'm pretty sure things would have turned out differently."

I squeeze Aiden's arm. "I'm sorry, Aiden. I wish I could have met her."

"She was a kind woman. I know that she would have accepted Elaine's mate without question." He sighs. "What I'm trying to say is I love you with every ounce of my being. Our love can change things. It has power."

Tears prickle my eyes hearing him tell me that. "I love you too." The words escape my lips before I can even think about it because it's the truth. My heart is utterly lost to him after only four days together. All of me is lost to this shifter whose arms feel like home.

He smiles and twirls me around, kissing me softly. "Then trust me. I'd do anything to protect you and get your family back." He kisses me again. "I'll do anything to make amends for the crimes my father committed."

I melt into him as he continues to kiss me softly and passionately.

He breaks away and searches my eyes. "When do you want to attempt this?" he asks.

"As soon as possible. You heard Flynn, they are alive, for *now*."

He nods. "We'll go right away, but first, I need to ask Flynn to get his men ready. We will free your family and then go and reclaim my castle." Aiden glances at me, and his eyes scan across my clothes. "You need to wear something protective."

I tilt my head to the side. "I don't have anything."

He smiles. "You're a witch. Conjure something."

"Good point." I focus my power into creating some leather armor. We might have to fight the guards if they don't accept Aiden as their king and leader now.

My magic has felt more powerful ever since I met Aiden. I can feel it getting stronger inside of me by the day. It burns around me and encases me in brown leather armor with gilt detailing and a cloak.

"Wow, you look amazing," Aiden says, eyes flooding with desire.

I twirl around. "Thank you." I stop and stare at him. "Why do we need to break in there when you are the king now?"

He shrugs. "The guards won't know I'm king or that I'm even aware the place exists."

I smile as an idea comes to my mind.

"What's the smirk for?"

"I've got a plan."

He grabs my hand and pulls me into his chest. "I get a feeling I'm not going to like this plan."

"You are the king now. If you approach the prison with me as your prisoner for the camp, we'll get in easy. They can't deny you entry."

Aiden's eyes narrow. "Isn't it safer for me to burn them all to a crisp?"

"Surely we should give them a chance to do the right

thing. Your father ordered them, but he's dead. You're the king now, and they should listen to you."

He smiles at me.

"What's that look for?"

He shakes his head. "You are perfect."

My cheeks blaze on fire at his compliment. "How do you inform Flynn of the plan?"

He nods his head toward me.

My brow furrows. "What?"

"Conjure him, love. You're a witch, now start acting like one."

I swallow hard. The thought of conjuring a faerie makes me sick to the stomach. It's a sign of disrespect to conjure someone like that, especially a king.

I shake my head. "That's not a good idea. I'd rather send him a message."

Aiden lets out a huff but nods. If there's one thing I've learned about him in the past few days, he likes to get on with something. He hates planning and wants to jump headfirst into a task. It's a strength and a weakness.

I write down a note on a piece of paper and picture Flynn's face clearly in my mind. "In manibus," I mutter, and the paper bursts into flame and disappears.

"Now what?" Aiden asks.

I meet his gaze. "Now, we wait."

He looks disappointed. "I hate waiting around when I pumped to go."

I laugh. "Well, go fly it off, then."

He shakes his head. "No, I'm not leaving you alone."

I glare at Aiden, knowing that he's protective because he's my mate, but it's getting on my nerves. "Aiden, what do you think I did when you weren't around?" I ask, tilting my head to the left. "I live alone in San Francisco, and until four days ago, we'd never met. You need to stop with this."

He rubs a hand over the back of his neck. "I'm sorry, it's in my nature."

A flash of blue light catches my attention in the kitchen, and I rush in there. "Flynn, you got my message?"

He nods. "Of course, my men are on their way to the castle. They will stay hidden until we arrive." He smiles. "I intend to come with you."

I glance back at Aiden, who looks a little uncertain. "Are you sure that's a good idea?"

He nods. "Certain. I've heard rumors that your father kept fae locked in this prison too. If that's the case, having me with you will be a strength."

Aiden glances at me. "What do you think?"

I look back at Flynn. "I think the more help, the better. We've got no idea what we are walking into."

Flynn claps his hands. "I like this one. She's got the brains."

Aiden's eyes narrow. "Yes, she does."

"Shall we." Flynn holds out both his hands to us.

"What?" He tilts his head to the side. "Surely, we

will fly."

Flynn laughs. "I know a quicker and easier way than that. Trust me."

I want to trust this man, so I step up and take his hand first. It's impossible not to notice how Aiden's jaw clenches the moment he sees me touch another man. He's quick to take his other hand and set his free arm around my waist.

"Prepare yourselves," Flynn says, as suddenly the room begins to spin. He's dispersing with us. I knew all fae could disperse, but I didn't realize they could take passengers.

When we stop spinning, I bend over, trying to regain my bearings. My stomach twists with sickness. Once I stand again, I see we're at the base of a mountain.

"Couldn't you have taken us straight to the entrance?" Aiden asks.

Flynn shakes his head. "Not without knowing what it looks like, I'm afraid we're going to have to walk the rest of the way."

Aiden glances at me. "How is the plan going to work now? I was supposed to be bringing Ilsa as a prisoner."

Flynn smiles and clicks his fingers, clapping his wrists in iron. "Looks like you've got two prisoners now."

I stare up at the mountain, feeling my nerves increase. My parents and brother could be up there somewhere, being tortured. I hope to God that we get to them in time—the alternative is too hard to consider.

15

AIDEN

*I*lsa's plan is dangerous but genius, but Flynn being here makes me uneasy. There's no reason it shouldn't work. I find it hard to believe that the men guarding this prison haven't heard of my father's death.

The mountain looms in front of us as I try to stop my head from spinning from what Flynn forced upon us.

"Couldn't you have taken us straight to the entrance?" I ask.

Flynn shakes his head. "Not without knowing what it looks like, I'm afraid we're going to have to walk the rest of the way."

I glance at Ilsa, realizing we haven't even discussed what we're doing about Flynn. "How is the plan going to work now? I was supposed to be bringing Ilsa as a prisoner."

Flynn smiles and clicks his fingers, clapping his arms in iron. "Looks like you've got two prisoners now."

He's a quick thinker, I'll give him that. Flynn has been a help, and I trust him, but I still feel uneasy working so closely with a faerie.

Ilsa stares up at the mountain, clad in her sexy leather. She drives me wild with need, but I need to focus. It's going to be a tough trek, particularly for her.

I walk over to Ilsa, grabbing her wrists before she even notices me.

"What are you—"

I slap a pair of metal handcuffs on her wrists. "We have to make it believable. "

She licks her bottom lip slowly. "Why haven't you got these out before?" she breathes, thinking Flynn won't hear.

He chuckles behind me. "Yes, do tell, Aiden."

She turns bright red.

I smirk, not a bit embarrassed by Flynn overhearing. "Maybe I will, tonight." I nod toward the mountain. "Let's do this, love. Let's get your family back."

She smiles. "Okay." Her hand entwines with mine, and I glance down at it.

My stomach twists with nerves. As long as we find them alive, she'll have to explain our bond to then.

If they aren't, then I don't know what it will mean for us. Could Ilsa love a man whose father killed her family?

I swallow hard, feeling the fear rise inside of me—fear that I could lose her. It would end me.

"What's wrong?" she asks.

I shake my head. "Nothing."

Her brow furrows. "Aiden, don't lie to me." She squeezes my hand. "Tell me what is bothering you."

I nod, despite knowing I can't tell her the truth. I can't speak my worst fear in case it becomes reality. "What if your family doesn't approve of us?"

She laughs. "That's what you are worried about?"

Not exactly.

I'm worried your family isn't alive, but I keep that to myself.

She shakes her head. "It's not like I'm royalty. My parents have no say on who I have a relationship with." It doesn't make me feel any better. The fact is my father trapped them in a damn concentration camp.

Why would they be happy about his son mating to their daughter?

"Okay." I keep my hand in hers and start to walk, but she jolts me to a stop.

"Aiden, they will love you, anyway." She looks serious now. "My parents are the most open-minded people I know, trust me."

I smile. "Thanks, love." I kiss her softly.

Flynn clears his throat. "Very touching, but can we get on with it?" He raises a brow. "My men are waiting for us at the castle."

I nod and break away from Ilsa, staring up the looming mountain.

"You're sure the entrance is up there somewhere?"

Flynn nods. "Yes, I'd bet it will be near the summit, but I'm not sure."

Luckily, we're all fit, but I'm not sure Ilsa is used to hiking.

"Okay, let's go."

We head upward in silence until Flynn starts to hum. I try to ignore it as we head toward the halfway point.

I glance back and notice that Ilsa is struggling to keep up with both of us. We forget she's a witch, hardly stronger than a human in physical terms.

"Are you okay, love," I call back.

She quickens her pace and catches me up. "I think you forget that I'm no dragon shifter. I'm a witch and no faster than a human."

Guilt tears through me. "Sorry, I'll slow down." I encase her hand with mine and slow down my steps, glancing at Flynn. "Can you slow it down, Ilsa can't walk as fast as us."

He glances back and nods. "Of course, sorry, I struggle to walk at the speed of humans." He tilts his head. "And witches, it would seem."

We're only halfway up, and it's taking longer than I expected to get there. We're going to be caught out in the dark. It's okay if it's just us three, but I've got a feeling the number of witches and other beings we will be freeing will be ridiculous. I can't believe how blind I've been when it comes to my father's mental state.

We walk in silence, other than Flynn's constant humming.

There's a tension between Ilsa and me. It's unspoken, but we're both worried about what we will find in this prison.

After we're about three-quarters of the way up, I can feel my patience with Flynn's humming fading. "Do you have to hum?" I ask, glaring at the fae king.

He smirks and holds his hands up. "I'm sorry. I always find music is calming."

Ilsa nods. "I was enjoying it. What song is it?"

"An old, fae song called *Nádúr*. It means nature in my mother tongue."

The rest of the way, we walk in silence, until we come to a massive black metal gate carved into the rock. "This is it," I glance at both of them. "Both of you stay quiet, remember, you're prisoners."

"Who's there?" a voice calls from the gate which is glowing bright blue. It must be the enchantment that protects the place.

"Your king, Aiden Jeremiah, and I've got two prisoners."

The gates move open, and a man comes out through the blue magic. "Wow, I wasn't expecting to see you, ever, sir." He bows his head.

His brow furrows. "There's a rumor going around that you're dead."

I shake my head. "No, very much alive, and ready to take back my castle. I thought the enchantment kept all news out?"

He rubs a hand across his neck. "It's been weakening for a while, and we can get information in and out now." There's a tension in the air, which is palpable.

He glances back at the prisoners. "Come on in. My name is Jared, by the way."

I follow him into the dark tunnel carved out of the mountainside. Candles affixed to the wall light it dimly, but it's still very dark. I notice Ilsa squinting to try and see. Flynn and I have eyesight good enough to cut through this, but she doesn't.

"Your father told you about this place?" Jared asks.

I nod. "Yes, why wouldn't he?"

His brow furrows. "He told us you weren't on board. Even if he were to die, that we would have to continue his work in his name."

I feel the pain slice through me hearing that. My father wanted to pull the wool over my eyes in death. "What right would you have to disobey your king if I wanted this operation shut down?" I ask, glaring at him.

Jared pales. "None, sir." He bows his head. "I heard that Charles had claimed the throne."

I growl at him, feeling rage bubbling under the surface. Charles is vermin that I'm going to exterminate.

Ilsa's gives me a warning look.

"It's about time I taught you who your king is." I grab him suddenly by the collar, forcing him against the wall hard. Ilsa might be warning me to be cautious, but I have to assert my dominance. If these assholes think that I've been defeated, they are greatly mistaken.

"I'm shutting this bullshit down, as the current king didn't sanction it. Do you understand me?" I ask, allowing my dragon to rise to the surface. If he denies, I will tear him apart.

He nods. "Of course, but I thought you brought this witch and fae as a prisoner of the camp." He glances at Ilsa and then at Flynn.

"Change of fucking plan. I want you to release the witches and warlocks now."

Jared bites his bottom lip. "Just the witches and warlocks, sir?" he asks.

Flynn was right then. "Who else is kept captive here?"

His eyes widen. "Dragon shifters, wolf shifters, vampires, and a couple of faeries even." He glances at Flynn again.

Flynn clicks his fingers, and the restraints drop off his wrists. "I knew it, that bastard."

I shake my head. "How the fuck do you keep them all contained?" This complicates everything. Vampires kept in captivity will want to do nothing but get revenge, and I'm not sure wolf shifters will be much different. I'm not their king. They won't give a damn that I'm letting them go after my father tortured them.

The fae may be more accepting because I'm here with Flynn.

"Fuck," I growl. "Why was my father keeping our kind captive?"

He swallows hard. "Aiden, I think there is something you'll want to see."

Dread twists my gut, but I nod my head. "Fine, show me."

Ilsa squeezes my hand as we move, jolting me to a stop. "Aiden, I don't like this."

I smile at her. "Don't worry. I won't let anything happen to you or your family."

Jared leads me down a dark corridor and stops in front of a heavy wooden door. "Prepare yourself, Aiden." He slips the key into the lock and unlocks the door. It swings open to reveal a surprisingly lovely room.

I meet his gaze. "You go in first, please."

Jared nods and steps inside.

I glance back at Flynn. "Will you stand watch?"

"Of course, you can count on me." He winks.

I turn back to the room and enter with Ilsa just behind me, keeping a wary eye on Jared.

A figure sits by the window in an armchair. I can't make out who it is.

Jared clears his throat, and the figure looks our way. It feels like time slows to a stop as my mother unmistakably meets my gaze.

She won't recognize me. The last time she saw me, I was only ten years old. "Aiden?"

My heart skips a beat. "Mother?"

133

She stands up and rushes over to me. "Oh, my boy. I've missed you so much." She hugs me tightly.

I feel stunned, speechless.

How is this possible?

"W-What are you doing here?" I shake my head. "Father said you were dead. We buried you."

She pulls away and sets her hands on my arms. "Son, your father put me in here. He didn't like it when I stood up against his barbaric plan for this place, so he entrapped me."

It feels like my world is spinning into oblivion.

How could I have lived all these years so blind to the truth?

I stumble backward, but Ilsa is there. Her hands settle on my back. "Aiden, are you okay?"

I shake my head. "I can't believe it. All these years, I've let this happen right in front of my eyes."

My mother places her hands on either side of my chin and shakes her head. "It's not your fault, sweetheart. Your father is a master manipulator." Her brow furrows. "How did you find out about this place?"

I clear my throat, trying to get a grip on my emotions. "Flynn, the faerie king told me about it." I glance backward and know he's still waiting outside.

"Does your father know you are here?" she asks.

"He's dead. Killed by rebels."

My mother looks relieved to hear the news of my father's passing. All my life, I believed they were the epitome of true love. "How could father turn on you?" I shake my head. "His mate."

She sighs heavily. "Your father was sick, Aiden. He craved power beyond anything, and he was dead set on eliminating every species other than the dragon shifters." I watch her as she turns away and paces the floor. "It got to a point where I couldn't stand by him, not anymore."

I nod my head. "Even a mating bond isn't that strong."

There's a sad smile on her lips. "No. It's not."

I'm in turmoil as I try to process what I'm learning. My father faked my mother's death. All this time, I believed his anger and hatred was born out of the loss of her. He's the reason I lost her.

My mother steps toward me and sets her hand on my arm. "How is Elaine?"

Pain clutches at my chest, and I feel tears well up in my eyes. "She's dead."

My mother clutches at my arm, suddenly unsteady. "No. She can't be."

It makes it even crueler that she was alive only a week ago. Elaine struggled the most when we lost our mother. She hated my father, and now I can see why. I stood by his side, too blind to see what was going on right in front of my eyes.

"I'm sorry. I was too late to save her."

My mother's tears flood down her face as she weeps against me. "Oh, Aiden. Please tell me it wasn't your father who killed her."

I shake my head. "No, rebels." I clench my fists by

my side. "Charles was behind her death."

My mother steps backward, eyes wide. "Charles Anderson?"

"Yes, I'm starting to think I'm the worst judge of character ever. How can I be king?" I turn around, and I meet Ilsa's gaze. She's been quietly waiting behind me as I reunite with my mother.

"You'll be a stronger, better king than your father ever could have been," my mother says, stepping to my side. She notices Ilsa. "Who is this?"

I swallow hard and beckon Ilsa forward.

She gives me a hesitant look.

"This is Ilsa, my mate."

My mother's face lights up. "Oh, wonderful. Come here, dear." She holds out her hand.

Ilsa looks uncertain but moves forward. "It's nice to meet you, your highness." She bows her head slightly.

My mother laughs. "None of the nonsense. Call me, Eleanor." She takes Ilsa's hand. "I'm glad his father is no longer here. He wouldn't have been happy about your pairing." She glances at me. "You know he would have tried to kill her, don't you?"

I didn't know that until this moment. It feels like I didn't know the man who raised me at all. His darkness goes beyond anything I believed. Dragon shifters tend to lean toward the dark, but I never expected him to be this evil and heartless.

"I do now," I say, running a hand through my hair.

"I'm here to shut this operation down and free Ilsa's family."

My mother smiles. "That's my boy." She cups my face again. "I knew you were too good to be poisoned by that man's hate."

I take Ilsa's hand in mine and meet her gaze. "Let's go and find your family."

The beautiful smile that twists onto her lips threatens to break me entirely. All I want to do is wrap this woman up in cotton wool and never let her go.

She's too precious to me to be risking in a place like this. All I can hope is that her family is unharmed. Otherwise, I don't know what it means for us and our future.

16

ILSA

*T*he guard leads us down a dark corridor.

Flynn trails close behind with Aiden's mother. "It's great to meet you, Eleanor. I admired your work before your faked death."

I glance back to see her smiling. "It's nice to meet you too, Flynn."

How can they both be so at ease?

I guess they aren't about to find out if their family is alive. It's hard to believe that Aiden's father could have made a place as terrible as this, knowing his son.

A scream pierces the air, and I feel my heart rate spike. Aiden and I exchange glances.

He clears his throat. "I did say I want an end to everything that is happening here." He glares at Jared. "I meant immediately."

Jared pales and fumbles for the radio on his belt. "Of course, sir." He presses the button. "Kegan tell everyone that the new king is here. All operations are halted."

"Holy shit, are you serious?" The guy on the other end comes through.

"Yeah, stop everything now." Jared's voice is laced with panic as he glances warily at Aiden.

"Roger that."

He visibly relaxes the moment the other guy agrees. "The witches are kept in the cells ahead." He glances at me. "Is there someone in particular you are looking for?"

Aiden steps in front of me. "Don't address her directly."

I set a hand on Aiden's arm. "It's fine. Yes, my family."

"Can you supply me with their names?"

I nod. "Irene, Rowan, and Eric."

Jared pales. "Right, I-I."

A flood of panic hits me at his reaction. They can't be dead. I won't accept that my mate's father ripped away my family forever.

"What's the problem, Jared?" Aiden asks.

He shakes his head. "They are alive, but…" He swallows hard. "It's best you see for yourself. Follow me."

Relief floods me hearing they are alive, but I can't understand what could be so bad that he's not telling us. My stomach twists as we move deeper and deeper into the belly of the mountain. The darkness seems to increase with every step.

Jared stops outside a massive oak door and digs his hand into his pocket for the key.

I watch as he slips it inside and then turns the lock, swinging the door open. A white glow filters out of the room and into the dark corridor. I'm eager to look inside and step forward.

Aiden grabs my hand, jerking me to a stop. "You don't know what you are walking into, love, stay behind me."

I pull my hand away and set them on my hips. "Aiden, this is my family, and I'll do what the hell I want." I move past him before he can say another word and slip into the room.

I hear his mother chuckle. "I like that one, Aiden. She's got fire."

I step into the room. My heart stops beating when I see my brother's face first. He's unconscious, pale, and floating in mid-air. Then I see my mom and dad next to him. They're all hooked up to a machine—a machine I've heard horrific rumors about.

It's a magic harnessing machine, draining them of their powers and slowly killing them.

My mom and dad look like they've still got color in their face, but my brother Eric is too pale.

"Get them off of it *now*," I cry, panic clutching at my heart.

Jared swallows hard. "I'm afraid the only person

who knew the code to stop the machine was Aiden's father, and he is…"

"Dead," Aiden finishes the sentence off for him.

Jared nods. "Your father may have written it down somewhere at the castle," he suggests.

"Do they even have enough time for us to claim back the castle and then search it?"

Jared shrugs. "Everyone is different. Some last for weeks, while others only days."

Aiden shakes his head. "What the fuck was my father trying to achieve with this?"

Flynn clears his throat. "I've got a feeling this was our answer to how they are keeping so many powerful beings' captive here."

"They're magic is being used to keep them locked up?"

Aiden's mother sets a hand on his shoulder. "Yes, and I've got a feeling I know where we will find the code to stop the machine." She narrows her eyes at Jared. "You do have a way to slow it down, though, don't you?"

He bows his head. "Yes, your majesty. I'll do that now." He walks over to a control station and starts to fiddle with the dials.

The glowing light around the witches and warlocks reduces.

She glances at me. "Don't worry, dear, we'll get your family out of here, alive." Her confidence is infectious, but I am worried about my brother. He's always been the strongest physically, and his face tells me he is fading fast. It's shocking to see.

"We had best get a move on then, as my brother isn't looking good."

I notice other witches and warlocks strung up, looking worse than my brother. It's such an injustice that I struggle to get my head around what kind of man my mate's father could have been.

He lured them under pretenses and did this to them. I can't understand what he was trying to achieve by draining witches and warlocks magic to hold other beings' captive.

"Yes, it's time for me to take back the castle," Aiden says, his eyes pure dragon.

He looks fearsome with his fists clenched and eyes almost glowing. As I stare at him, I try to come to terms with the fact that he came from a man capable of this.

Does that mean he has it in him to be as evil?

I try to push that thought from my mind. Aiden isn't his father. He cares about people and doesn't believe in segregation. The pledge at the council meeting proved that much.

"Let's go then," I say, taking one last glance at my family.

They have to hold on until we make it back. I can't lose them.

THE CASTLE LOOMS OVER US. Dark, grey clouds dot the sky as a crash of thunder rumbles nearby.

Behind us, a small army of fae warriors is ready to charge Aiden's home.

Flynn steps to my side and smiles at me. "There's nothing to worry about. They won't even hear us coming."

Aiden nods at Flynn. "Remember, Charles is mine."

Flynn nods. "Of course, I wouldn't have it any other way."

Aiden grips my hand. "You don't need to come inside. It's going to be dangerous."

I shake my head. "I'm a witch, Aiden. I think you forget that I can take care of myself."

His mother steps up to his other side. "Let the girl be, Aiden." She gives me a warm smile. I know we are going to get along, even though we've just met. "We go in as a family and face whatever is waiting for us on the other side."

Aiden nods and releases my hand. The loss of warmth makes me shiver as I stare up at the stone building.

If Flynn is right, the man who took over the castle is Aiden's childhood friend. He wants to fight Charles, but I can't help feel it will hurt him too much.

Flynn glances at Aiden. "Shall we head in first?"

Aiden nods. "Yes, round up the shifters who opposed me. If you can avoid killing, do so."

Flynn smiles. "As always, fae don't kill unnecessarily."

I raise my brow, as I've heard such different things in the stories. Perhaps that's because that's all they are, fictional stories.

We watch as Flynn and his army move silently toward the door, unlocking it and opening it at unbelievable speed.

Aiden takes the first step up to the entrance, but I grab his arm. "Are you sure you should face Charles?"

He nods his head. "There's no one else who can. Trust me, love." He glances at his mother. "Are we ready?"

She nods, and he meets my gaze. I'm not sure I am, but I have to face this. We're a team now, and the shifters inside the castle are opposed to my mate. I'll do anything to get him back where he belongs.

"Ready as I'll ever be."

Aiden smiles and then continues to walk forward, heading for the castle eagerly. I follow him, feeling stronger than ever. My power has been building ever since we met, and now I know why our coven's power is so low. King Kendall was sucking the life out of hundreds of witches and warlocks.

Aiden stops in front of the door and turns back to us. "Follow my lead. We all stick together inside, do you understand?"

His mother waves a hand in the air. "Aiden, I'm your

mother, not one of your subjects. Let's get on with it and burn that bastard, Charles, to a crisp."

I swallow hard as Aiden nods and turns back and steps through into the castle hallway. It's deathly silent. I wonder if the fae warriors have even started rounding up the traitors yet.

I follow him next, and his mother is right behind me. "I don't like this," I breathe, glancing around the empty hallway.

Aiden shakes his head. "Come on. I think I know where he will be."

His mother clears her throat. "Aiden, you need to find Charles, but I need to find that passcode."

She's right. We will do better if we split up, but Aiden doesn't want to.

"It's too dangerous to split up. What if Charles finds one of us alone?"

His mother smiles. "I think you forget how powerful a shifter your mother is, son." Her brow raises. "Not to mention, this castle is crawling with a hundred fae warriors to protect me."

He grits his teeth. "Fine. Be careful. I've just found you. I don't want to lose you too."

She shakes her head. "Don't worry. You won't." She steps up to him and hugs him before taking my hand and squeezing. "I'll find that passcode for your family, dear."

I smile. "Thank you."

We watch her walk up the stairs, disappearing. Once

she's gone, I turn my attention back to Aiden. "What's the plan?"

Aiden's eyes flash with uncertainty. "Charles has a favorite part of this castle. I bet any money he is there right now."

"Where?" I ask.

He glances at a door at the back of the grand hallway that leads outside. "The maze in the garden."

My brow furrows. "Why would he be in the maze?"

Aiden's jaw clenches. "He will know I'm here."

"How?"

He shakes his head. "Not all those guards will be loyal to me at the prison, and he would have scented me before I entered."

"The maze is the perfect place to hide." He grabs my hand. "Come on. We're going to find him now."

I let Aiden guide me out of the back of the castle into a huge, landscaped garden. A giant hedge maze sits in the center. Aiden heads straight for it, but I pull him to a stop. "Do we have a plan?" I ask, eyeing it suspiciously.

He shakes his head. "How can we plan for the unknown? Stick with me, and we'll be fine."

"Okay."

We head through the entrance of the thick, tall maze. Aiden clears his throat. "Charles, I know you are here. I can fucking smell you. Come out and face me," he shouts.

My eyes widen. I'm not sure it's a good idea to signal

where we are in the maze. An uneasy feeling clutches at my gut.

Suddenly, a young man appears in front of us. He's handsome, with dark black hair and dark brown eyes. "You came to face me, finally." He tilts his head. "What took you so long, Aiden?"

He growls a deep sound. "You're bastard, Charles. How could you betray me?"

He laughs. "Quite easily."

Aiden shakes his head. "Are you ready to fight fair? Dragon against Dragon?"

Charles tilts his head to the side slightly. "Sure, I'm the stronger one."

Aiden clenches his fists by his side and glances at me. "Stand back, love."

I take a few steps backward, knowing he's about to shift. He doesn't take the time to get undressed as he starts to shift into his dragon form.

His clothes rip apart as his scales begin to break out across his tan skin. I watch in awe as his clothes shred to pieces, left in a pile. I'll never get used to seeing him shift and change into a dragon.

Charles roars too, as black scales start to ripple across his skin. Black dragons are renowned for leaning toward the darkness the most, and they are scarce. Aiden should have been warier around him.

I guess it's easy to fall into a false sense of trust with someone you've known since you were a child.

They both square off against each other, eyes wild. I

take a few more steps backward and take cover behind a giant statue.

If they use fire, I'll be screwed. This maze will burn to the ground quickly. Aiden is strong, but I can't leave him to it. He might need a witch on his side. I watch with gritted teeth as they both rush toward each other, talons and teeth bared.

My heart is pounding against my rib cage as I watch them crash in an angry clash of talons and teeth. I've never felt more scared as I watch Charles sink his teeth into Aiden. This is going to be the most nerve-racking moment of my life.

17

AIDEN

I lunge for Charles with my talons, missing him by an inch. He tries to sink his sharp, razor teeth into my neck, but I'm too quick.

How did we come to this?

Best friends since we were kids, and now he wants to end me. I always knew he was jealous. He's always been in my shadow because of my royal status, but I never knew he hated me this much.

I feel the fire rising in my throat. It's building along with my rage. Not that it would help against Charles in his dragon form too. Perhaps I should have seen this coming. All black dragons are prone to falling from grace. Charles is the only one I know.

He swipes his talon across my face, cutting me. I roar and launch myself at him, catching him in the side. Thick, black blood oozes from the side of his abdomen as I catch an unarmored part of his belly. The screech that comes from him is enough to deafen most people, but not a dragon.

I think of Ilsa, hoping she is staying back. She is a distraction from the fight at hand. I need to keep her out of my mind.

Charles launches at me and catches my side too, slicing me with his sharp talon.

I twist and grab his neck between my razor-sharp teeth, shaking my head to break through the scales at the top of his neck.

He growls, trying desperately to get out of my grip. I will kill him, even if it kills me. This man murdered Elaine. I can't deny that I'm thankful he took my father out, after learning the truth about him.

Charles manages to break free and grabs hold of my arm with his sharp talons, digging them in deep.

I roar as black blood litters the ground. We're slowly tearing each other apart.

The screech of another dragon draws my attention. My mother—she's in her majestic emerald form.

A dragon on dragon fight is going to achieve nothing but both of our slow and painful deaths. If she can tip the scales, we can get him into a cell, and he will stand trial for treason.

We need to make a statement. Anyone who fucks with the royal family will answer for their crimes. She lands by my side and roars at Charles. His eyes widen as he recognizes her, clearly unaware that she was still alive.

It seems my father was good at keeping that fact hidden from most of the damn world, including me.

My mother launches herself at Charles and is quick to fasten her teeth around his throat, making him whimper as she latches on. He slices at her, but she hardly flinches.

I bound forward and slide my talon under his throat, ready to cut. I meet his gaze as he cowers lower to the ground, falling onto his knees.

He whimpers, before bowing his head in submission.

My mother lets go of his throat, and he slowly shifts back into his human form. He curls up on the ground, a shell of a man. Blood oozes from his wounds, as Ilsa comes out of her hiding spot.

"What are you going to do with him?" she asks, looking me straight in the eye.

I shift back to my human form, as does my mother. Ilsa blushes the moment I do, clearly uncomfortable by our state of undress. It's natural for us and not embarrassing, but I can understand why it would be for her.

"He will stand trial."

Ilsa waves her hand and summons two robes, throwing me one. She passes the other to my mother. "Here you go."

My mother glances at it hesitantly before taking it and wrapping it around herself.

"He won't last it to a trial with those injuries." Ilsa's eyes go to the slice in my stomach, and she rushes forward. "Let me heal you."

I wrap the robe around part of myself, keeping the wound visible. "It's a scratch." She shakes her head, holding her hand over the wound. "Et ad sanandum potentiam magia," she chants, as the magic tickles over my skin, sealing the wound. "There, as good as new." Her eyes go to the man on the ground. "Do I need to heal him, too?"

I grit my teeth as I stare down at the man who was once my best friend. I cared about Charles like a brother, and he took my sister from me. Elaine was innocent. She didn't deserve what he did to her.

Ilsa is right. He won't survive long enough to stand trial.

"Only heal some of them, to ensure he'll survive until the trial."

Ilsa meets my gaze and nods. "Okay." She squeezes my hand as she steps forward.

I watch as Charles remains still on the floor. He has barely moved since he shifted back into his human form.

She places her hands over his worst wound at the neck and chants her magic spell. Slowly, the injuries start to seal as the magic darts out over his skin.

I feel torn. We should leave Charles to die in this maze. He doesn't deserve a trial, but at the same time, I have a reputation to uphold.

Charles moves suddenly, grabbing Ilsa.

My heart skips a beat as the moonlight glints of the metal of a knife. Charles holds it up to her throat, making my stomach twist.

He smirks at me. "Always playing by the book, Aiden, it's the reason you are weak. You should have killed me when you had the chance." He shakes his head. "Your father knew it. That's why he appointed me to take over from him."

My stomach twists. "You killed my father," I spit.

His smirk widens. "Yes, he asked me to, he was ill and knew it was the best way to throw you in at the deep end. He knew the least prepared you were, the easier it would be for me to kill you."

It feels like nothing my father did could shock me, but it's worse now. I feel a flood of panic as he increases the pressure of the knife against Ilsa's throat.

One flick of his wrist and he could take everything I love away from me.

"Don't hurt her," I say.

He smirks. "Or what? It looks like you are the loser here, Aiden."

I notice Ilsa muttering something under her breath, but I keep my attention on Charles.

She has something up her sleeve.

Charles's knife is thrown into the air and floats toward me. Ilsa shoves him hard in the gut with her elbow, before turning around and punching him square in the face. She busted his nose with one hit, as he falls to the floor.

Before he can even move, Ilsa shouts, "Conligo."

A pair of metal cuffs clap on his wrists, and a tree

branch shoots out of the ground and binds his legs, holding him to the floor.

I feel so much pride as I stare at my mate. Ilsa doesn't need me to protect her. It's a ridiculously attractive quality, deepening my love for her more than I believed possible. Ilsa's the perfect equal to me—my queen, in every sense of the word.

I step forward and set my hands on her shoulders, pulling her close. "That was amazing, love."

She smiles at me. "I told you I don't need protecting."

My mother approaches. "You certainly don't." She sets her hand on my shoulder. "I found the passcode." She passes the paper into my hand."

Ilsa smiles widely. "How is Flynn getting on?"

"Perfectly well. All the traitors are rounded up and in the dungeons. We had a few dragon losses."

Ilsa practically jumps out of her skin as Flynn speaks behind her.

"Fuck, don't ever sneak up on me again like that," she says.

Flynn chuckles. "Sorry." His eyes land on the piece of paper in her hands. "It looks like it's time to go and free your family and the rest of the prisoners."

Ilsa nods. "Yes, let's do this." She holds her hand out willingly to Flynn.

I can't help my jaw tighten every time I see her touch another man. It's the possessiveness of the bond, even though I know Flynn isn't a threat.

My mother links hands with Flynn on his other side. I take their hands and brace myself.

I hate fucking traveling by dispersing, but I can't deny it's efficient. Also, time is vital when it comes to getting Ilsa's family off that machine. We start to spin, and blue lights flood my vision as I tighten my grip on Ilsa's hand and my mother's. I can't believe she's alive.

The two most important women in my life are here with me. I just wish Elaine could have been here too.

We touch down outside the gate of the prison, and Jared is on the watch. "Wow, that was fast."

I nod. "Yeah, we've got the passcode. Take us back to the machine."

He bows his head. "Of course, sir."

I walk ahead of the rest, holding Ilsa's hand as I go. I'm so thankful her family is still alive. I hope that machine hasn't done any irreversible damage to them.

Ilsa's tension is unmissable and I can practically smell her anxiety in the air. It's strange considering she's about to be reunited with her family.

18

ILSA

My heart is pounding so hard, it feels like it's going to beat out of my chest any minute. I watch Aiden's mother walk over to the control panel set out in front of my unconscious family.

Nerves flutter around in my stomach as I watch her punch in the passcode.

I hope to God that they have got off unscathed from being drained for over a week.

The horror stories I've heard about draining machines are awful. They can drive the witches or warlocks hooked up to them insane or make them lose their memories. I swallow hard, hoping they all recognize me once they are off of it.

An insane witch or warlock is a dangerous one. I can't stand to think about having to stop one or all of my family members after coming this far to find them.

Slowly, the machine starts to shut down. I watch,

wondering how long it will take for them to regain consciousness.

Aiden's father planned to destroy the world as we know it. It's hard to believe he's the son of a mastermind criminal. Yet, I look at his mother and know she's why he's the man he is today.

His father may have snatched her away from him early, but he has taken after her anyway.

Aiden sets a hand gently on my waist. "Are you okay?"

I glance up at him and smile. "Yes, nervous. I've heard some horror stories about machines like this and what it can do to witches that come off of them."

Aiden squeezes my hip softly. "Don't worry. They will be okay."

I shake my head. "You can't be sure of that."

He shrugs. "It's just a feeling I've got."

The darkness floods the room as the machine switches off entirely and the thud of bodies hitting the safety mat echo around us. I click my fingers, illuminating the room. They are still unconscious but lying on the soft mats beneath where they'd been floating. "How long will it take for them to wake?"

Jared, who is standing behind us, steps forward. "It can be anywhere between twenty minutes to two hours."

"Thank you, Jared. Can you get your men to come and take all of them somewhere more comfortable?" He glances back at me. "I think it's time for my queen and me to free the rest of the prisoners in this place."

Jared smiles. "Of course."

Aiden laces his fingers with mine. "We are going to come across some angry people, but we need to explain what happened."

Aiden's mother clears her throat. "Not without me, you don't."

Aiden laughs. "Of course not, mother. Officially, you are queen."

She shakes her head. "I'm too old for that." She waves her hand. "I want to live the rest of the life I've got since I've been trapped for twenty years."

It's impossible not to notice the guilt on Aiden's face. He may not have told me, but I know he blames himself for not learning sooner about his father's true nature.

Flynn clears his throat. "Don't forget me. I think the faeries may be easier to tame with me there."

Aiden nods. "Of course, I'm forever in your debt for this, Flynn."

Flynn shakes his head. "Consider it paid the moment you joined the council."

Aiden nods. "Thank you." He squeezes my hand. "Let's go and do this then. My father has wrongly imprisoned these people for far too long."

He pulls me out of the room, but I glance back at my family. All I want to do right now is wait with them until they wake.

Aiden senses my hesitation. "What's wrong, love?"

"I want to be there for them when they wake."

"You will be, this won't take any longer than twenty minutes."

I glance back at my parents and brother's lifeless bodies, before nodding. "Okay, I just can't wait to speak to them." Aiden smiles. "I know. Have patience, love." He guides me out of the corridor, and we all follow Jared to see the rest of the prisoners. Several men filter into the room to move all the witches as we leave.

I'm worried that we are going to face dangerous people in this prison. The thought of any more danger today makes me want to turn around and wait with my family, but now I'm with Aiden, I'm going to have more responsibilities than I could ever imagine.

As he says, I'm his queen now—the queen of the dragon shifters. That alone is dangerous. Dragons won't accept a witch as a queen willingly.

Jared glances back at us. "All species are in one main cell. It was only the witches and warlocks kept apart to use on the machine."

I meet Jared's eyes. "How many witches have died in here?"

A flash of fear enters his eyes. "Countless have died... I'm sorry, I don't know a figure."

I shake my head. "Estimate then. A thousand, ten thousand, hundreds of thousands. You must know a rough number."

He swallows hard. "Over the ten years I've been working this place, it would be in the hundreds of thousands."

His answer bowls me over. "How long has this place existed?"

Aiden's mother answers, "At least twenty years, that's how long I've been here."

Jared nods. "About twenty-five years in total, I believe. This place is the sole reason for the witches' loss of power."

Anger rises inside me. It's the reason why we've been weak and driven close to extinction. I can't wait to leave it and never come back.

Jared stops in front of a door and grabs a key out of his jacket pocket. "Brace yourself for this." His brow furrows. "They're not going to be happy. "

Jared swings open the door to a giant dungeon room full of people. As we enter, they all stare up at us and smirks curl onto some of their lips.

One vampire shouts out. "Pretty fucking risky to come in here while we're not behind a magic screen."

Aiden holds his hands up. "My father captured you and put you in here. I did not know this place existed until he died a week ago. I'm now king, and I wish to set you all free. Dragon shifters are going to be ruled differently in harmony with the fae and all other species." He signals at Flynn, who steps forward.

"Aiden and I have worked together to free you today. We have high hopes for the future and integration amongst the species."

There's a stunned silence. Even the vampire looks

surprised. "Are you saying we're all free to go, just like that?"

Aiden nods. "Yes, any grievances my father had with any of you have been forgotten. A clean slate. "

A few cheers break out, and Aiden nods to Jared to open up the doors entirely. There are about five going into the vast room that exit onto a lower level. They all come up. "Please go and return to your lives. I will do all I can to make amends in the years I'm the king."

From the looks on some of their faces, they aren't going to let go being kept captive so easily. Even so, they turn and leave. King Kendall's actions will mean Aiden will have to look over his shoulder while he's king—both of us will.

Jared clears his throat. "Well handled, sir. What about us now?"

Aiden tilts his head slightly.

The guards were doing their jobs, so he can't punish them for that.

"You will have positions in the king's guard should you want them. If not, you are welcome to leave."

Jared smiles. "I'd be honored to join the king's guard." He bows his head. "Thank you, sir. I'll pass on the information to the rest of the men here." He leaves in search of the rest of the guards.

Aiden turns to me. "Time to reunite you with your family."

I smile. "Yeah, and you've got to meet them."

He looks uncertain. "I should let you see them first, maybe later—"

"No, I want you with me, Aiden."

His Adam's apple bobs as he swallows, before allowing me to pull him out of the vast prison.

Flynn clears his throat. "I will see you all at the next meeting. I must return to my home."

I smile widely at the fae king. He isn't at all like I expected. "Thank you, Flynn. Thank you for everything."

He nods. "You're welcome." Suddenly he's engulfed in royal blue lights and disappears.

A guard walks down the corridor. "Where are the witches?" I ask.

He nods behind him at the door we'd gone through to find Aiden's mother. I enter the room to find a couple of witches I don't know sitting on chairs, head in their hands.

My brother is awake and sitting on the side of a bed with his head in his hands. My parents are still unconscious on that bed.

"Eric," I say his name, and he looks up at me, eyes widening.

"Ilsa, you found us." He stands, wobbling a little on his feet.

I rush toward him and wrap my arms around him. "You're okay. Do you remember everything?" I pull back and look into his eyes.

He runs a hand across the back of his neck. "Yeah,

although my memories of getting here are a little fuzzy. That bastard, King Kendall, lured us here."

I hug him again. "I know, but he died not long after. I came searching for you when you didn't come home."

He glances over at Mom and Dad's lifeless bodies. "Are they going to wake up?"

I grab his hand and squeeze. "Yes, the machine has only been turned off for twenty minutes. It can take up to two hours for them to wake up."

His attention goes behind me, and I know he's noticed Aiden. "Who is that guy staring at us?"

I glance back, smiling at Aiden. "Come on." I hold my hand out.

He walks forward and takes it.

"This is Aiden, my mate."

My brother's eyes widen. "What?" He shakes his head. "B-But, he's... I-"

"Yeah, I'm a dragon shifter." He holds his hand out to my brother. "Nice to meet you, Eric."

He looks at Aiden's hand with uncertainty before grabbing it and shaking. "Nice to meet you. "

They shake for a few moments before letting go. Eric often tried to act protective of me.

Aiden nudges me in the side. "Your mom is waking."

Eric and I rush over to her side, and I grab her hand. "Mom, are you okay?"

Her eyes flutter open, and she groans. "It feels like I've been put in a blender on the highest setting."

Dad groans by her side. "Tell me about it."

I smile, as they both struggle to sit up. "Ilsa, how are you here?" Mom asks when she finally gets a handle on her consciousness.

"When you guys didn't return, I had to come looking for you."

My mom's eyes widen. "That was dangerous. You could have ended up a prisoner. How did you find this place?"

I sigh. "It's a long story, and I'll tell it to you in full later." I glance back at Aiden and hold my hand out. "First, I'd like to introduce you to someone."

Aiden steps forward and takes my hand.

"Mom and Dad, this is Aiden, and he's—"

"The son of the man that locked us in here." She shifts further away on the bed. "Ilsa, that man is dangerous."

I shake my head. "Aiden helped me find you. He's my mate, and he did not know of this place."

My mom looks a little wary as she narrows her eyes at him. "Mate? Witches don't have mates."

I shake my head. "No, but dragons do. He found me, and we saved everyone in here together."

Aiden offers his hand. "It's lovely to meet you."

She shakes his hand and nods slightly. It makes sense that she would be wary of any dragon shifter after what his father did to them. I'm sure in time they will come to love him as much as I do.

It's insane the speed at which our love has blossomed, but I guess that's what happens when you are soul mates. Our destinies have been bound by fate before we even knew each other.

My dad shoves his hand forward. "Good to meet you, son."

I don't miss the flash of pain in Aiden's eyes at the word choice. He has recently lost his father and then found out he wasn't the man he knew. It must be hard. He takes my dad's hand and shakes. "You too, sir."

My dad raises a brow at the *sir.* A dragon king calling a random warlock sir is a bit odd, but I guess one day, he might be his father in law.

The thought makes my stomach twist, as I never saw myself as the marrying type. However, royalty always marries. Aiden's mother joins us. "Looks like we're all going to be one family."

"H-How, what... I-" My mom looks utterly shocked as she stammers in front of the queen. She shakes her head. "Everyone believed you were dead twenty-years ago."

Eleanor nods. "Indeed, thanks to my dear husband. He faked my death and locked me away, too much of a wimp to finish me off." Eleanor's eyes fill with tears. "I just wish Elaine had been here to be part of all of this. She would have loved it."

Aiden puts an arm around her. "She would have. I'm sorry, I was too late."

She shakes her head. "It's not your fault Aiden. Enough of that, let us be thankful for what we do have. I think a celebration at the castle is in order."

165

I smile as she turns away. My family stares after her in shock. There's going to be a lot of people confused by her reappearance. Her burial was a very publicized event because her death was suspicious.

Aiden's arm snakes around me instantly, naturally. I look up at the man I'm sure to spend the rest of my life with. He makes me feel warm and fuzzy inside. A feeling I've never felt before, but I never want it to stop.

19

AIDEN

I open the door and step into my bedroom, stopping in awe of the sight in front of me. Ilsa is standing in front of the mirror, entirely naked.

She jumps when she notices me and spins around, shaking her head. "You scared me half to death, Aiden."

My eyes wander down her beautiful body, relishing the sight. It's hard to believe we've only known each other a month.

The rebellion in the north is no longer since the death of Charles. He was the reason for all of the hardship that has fallen our kind since it started eight years ago, along with my father.

"What are you thinking?" Ilsa asks as she wraps a robe around herself, hiding her stunning body from me.

I narrow my eyes at her. "Take that off, *now.*"

She smirks at me and runs a finger across the bare

skin over her collarbone. "I'm not sure what you are talking about."

I growl at her teasing and rush toward her.

She giggles as I crash into her, ripping the fabric from her body.

"Don't push me, love."

"Or what, Aiden? Are you going to punish me?" There's a hint of excitement in her tone. We've been pushing the boundaries together day by day.

"Do you want me to?" I breathe, my lips inches from hers.

Her eyes search mine before she answers. "Yes."

I meld my lips to hers in a hot, desperate kiss, before bringing my hands down to her firm ass cheeks. I spank them, making her gasp. "If you want me to punish you, then I will." I bite her bottom lip softly. "But, are you forgetting about dinner?"

She glances over at the clock. "We still have half an hour."

I raise a brow. "This is going to take much longer than that." I lift her in my arms and carry her over to the desk in the corner of my bedroom. "Bend over," he says.

She bites her bottom lip before slowly bending over the desk.

I take a step back, enjoying the view—she is perfection.

My hand slowly traces the curve of her buttocks before moving to her back.

She gasps as I slowly move my hands across her skin, dragging out the anticipation.

I move my hand back to her full ass and spank softly.

She moans, arching her back and spreading her legs wider.

My cock throbs in my tight boxer briefs as I tease my hand between her thighs. She's soaking wet—she always is.

I spank her softly there, before moving back to her ass cheeks. The desire to paint her olive skin a pretty pink sends me wild. I spank her right ass cheek firmly first, three times.

She bucks her hips with each spank, getting needier.

I move to her left ass cheek and do the same, before kneeling and kissing her there.

"Oh, God, Aiden," she moans, digging her fingertips into the wood of the desk.

She glances over her shoulder back at me, eyes filled with hunger. Her desperation is on another level, as she digs her nails into my desk. I move my fingers between her thighs, brushing the sensitive skin either side of her perfect pussy. Her body visibly trembles in anticipation, as I move them slowly higher and higher to where she wants them.

I halt only an inch away from her, making her whimper.

"Aiden, please."

I spank her ass cheeks again. "That's it, love, beg

me." I kiss her pink skin on her ass before moving my fingers back to her inner thighs.

She jolts when I finally slide my fingers into her dripping wet entrance, groaning as I feel how wet she is. A satisfying moan comes from her lips, sending move desire south. It's almost impossible to control myself around this woman, but I love nothing more than making her needy.

I begin to move my finger in and out of her, pushing her higher. She's so wet that the sound of my finger sliding in and out of her fills the room. I rub my thumb over her clit in slow, lazy circles, trying to drive her insane.

She makes a frustrated sound, before finally snapping. "Please, Aiden, fuck me, now," she pants, watching me over her shoulder.

I shake my head. "No, love. I'm not finished punishing you."

She makes a move to glance at the clock. "What about the—"

I spank her ass harder this time. "Don't question me." I move back to get another good look at her dripping wet arousal. "So beautiful," I groan, gripping my hard length through my pants.

Ilsa gasps as I pull her clit into my mouth, sucking on it suddenly. Her thighs visibly shake, and I know if I'm not careful, I'll send her over the edge too quickly.

I lick a path through the center of her pussy, making her moan. "You taste so fucking sweet," I growl.

My control is slipping through my fingers as her scent goads my dragon to the surface. As I lick her pussy, delving my tongue as deep as it can go, I move my finger gently in circles over her clit.

She shudders, and I know she's getting close the way her muscles tighten around my finger.

I move my tongue to circle her clit and add another finger into her pussy. She groans as I stretch her more with two fingers, sending her higher with each thrust.

Whenever we're together, it feels like everything fades to the background. We have got a dinner to attend with the council members and our family. We're the damn hosts, but I can't drag myself away from her. We were doomed the moment I stepped in here and found her naked.

Her body shudders, and her muscles clamp down around my fingers. "Oh, God, Yes," she cries out.

I don't let up, guiding her through it and licking every drop of her sweet, honeyed juice. "That's it, love, come for me." I spank her ass again, as she comes undone.

I stand and slide my arm around her waist, pulling back against my clothed chest. I let my fingers move to her erect, hard nipples, and toy with them. "You are amazing."

Her eyes roll back in her head as I press my clothed cock into her pink, stinging ass cheeks.

"Are you ready for me now?" I ask, kissing a path down her neck to her shoulders.

171

She nods her head. "Please, I need you inside of me, Aiden."

I'll never get tired of her begging me for my cock. It drives me wild. I reach for the zipper between us and pull it down. I free my cock from my pants and push her back down over the desk. "Naughty girls get fucked over the desk hard," I growl.

She gasps as I keep my weight on her and keep her pressed against the hardwood surface.

I run the tip of my cock through her wetness. My dragon wants to lose control and fuck her hard and fast, but I want to drag this out. I want to make her crazy for me.

She arches her back in an attempt to push my cock inside of her.

I grab her hips hard and stop her from moving. "Stay still, love, or you will be waiting longer."

Ilsa whimpers and then stops moving, waiting patiently like a good girl.

"That's it, love. You know I'm in control. "

She groans as I let an inch of my cock slip inside of her. I don't go any further. "Stop teasing me, Aiden."

I smile, and my dragon indulges as I slide every inch deep into her.

Ilsa moans a satisfying moan, bucking her hips.

I'm not sure if she thinks I won't notice the movement if it's not hard, but she's greatly mistaken. I tighten my grip on her hips, digging my fingertips into them hard enough to bruise. "I told you not to move, love."

A frustrated sigh escapes her, but she doesn't complain.

I move in and out of her, feeling my dragon's impatience building too. All that's on his mind is getting his mate pregnant. That's been the case ever since I was deep inside of her that night in our cabin.

The thought of seeing Ilsa's belly growing round with my baby inside makes me crazy. I start to fuck her hard and deep.

Ilsa moans softly, loving everything I give her.

"Fuck, baby, you are so tight," I grunt as the muscles in her pussy grip me hard.

She's moving toward climax already. I just made her come only a few minutes ago.

I spank her pink ass, painting it a darker pink.

"Yes, Aiden, just like that," she moans, arching her back more.

My cock is as deep as it can go with every thrust, but it's like she wants it harder and faster. The woman is insatiable.

I feel my dragon rising, as my control on the reins slip.

Ilsa digs her nails into the desk, as I start to fuck her more roughly.

I slip my arm around her stomach, pull her back into my naked chest, and move in and out of her deeply. My lips move across her shoulder and neck, making her needier.

"Oh, God, Aiden."

"That's it, baby. I want you to come all over my cock."

She starts to shake in my arms as I let my teeth sink softly into her shoulder. I feel her tumble over the edge, as her pussy clamps down hard on my shaft. It feels like she's milking me for all I've got.

"Fuck," I roar as I explode deep inside of her, marking her as mine with my seed. She's mine, and she knows it, but everyone else would if she was big and round with my baby.

It's all I want—to start a family with the woman I love. A family that will be all about love and acceptance —the opposite of what my father provided Elaine and me.

We are both panting as we come down from our mutual climax. "Oh, look at that, right on time, love." I glance at the clock.

She punches me softly in the arm. "I can't go straight down. I need to shower."

I shake my head, hating the idea of her washing my mark off of her. "No way. We don't have time, and we're the hosts." I pull her into me. "I don't want you washing me off you."

Her cheeks turn a deep red. "But Flynn and Rhys will smell you on me."

I nod. "Exactly, and everyone will know you're *mine.*"

She lets out a sigh, but nods. "Fine, you're so overly possessive." She rolls her eyes.

"You love it, really." I fiddle with the box in my

jacket pocket, knowing that this is going to be unnerving. Proposing, in general, is nerve-racking, but maybe worse in front of family and friends.

My mom insists it is a royal tradition to propose to your future wife at a gathering. I'm not sure it's what Ilsa would want. She hates all the attention on her.

Ilsa slips into a stunning lace embellished red dress that matches the color of my scales. She's mesmerizing. "Will you do me up?" she asks, spinning around.

I smile, knowing she's only asking to feel me close to her. I've seen her do up countless dresses with her magic. "Sure, love." I step forward and let my fingers tease her skin before slowly doing up the zip. "All done. Shall we make an appearance at our own party now?"

She smiles at me. "If we must."

I lace my fingers in hers and lead her out of the room and down toward the ballroom—the room where I first set eyes on her. It is the perfect place to propose to her—the place we first saw each other—the place where our crazy journey started, and it's only just beginning.

Ilsa looks magnificent on my arm as we step into the ballroom.

Everyone is already here. Flynn gives me a nod as I enter. I never thought I'd have such an easy friendship with a faerie, but I owe him everything. Without him, I wouldn't have found Ilsa's family or my mother.

The entire council is here as well as our family and friends. I feel uneasy when I meet Vladimir's gaze. I can't deny I'm surprised when I see a human woman on his arm.

My stomach twists as I wonder if she's one of these blood bags they lure into their clutches. Rumor has it that some humans are stupid enough to volunteer themselves as blood bags, hoping that they will find a way to be turned into vampires.

It's not illegal, because the humans are willing. If they wish to leave, they can.

"Thank you all for coming to our party. I hope you have a good time."

A few people cheer and most clap as we come down the steps onto the main dance floor.

I give Vladimir a wide birth as the guy gives me the creeps and head toward Flynn first. He holds his hand out to me. "Good of you to turn up to your party."

I take his hand and shake it. "Sorry, we lost track of time." I glance at Ilsa. She turns bright red.

"I'm sure you did. Don't worry, Lucy and I have been in the same position as you. A month together." He sighs. "Those were the days."

Lucy clears her throat as she approaches. "What are you talking about, Flynn?"

Ilsa hugs Lucy, and I kiss her hand as a greeting. "Lovely to see you both again, and who is this?" I ask as a little boy with glowing blue eyes stares up at me.

"This is Killian, and..." Lucy searches behind her. "Niamh, come and greet our hosts." A young girl comes rushing over. "And, this is Niamh."

"A pleasure to meet you both," I say, crouching down and shaking Killian's hand before kissing Niamh's hand.

I stand up and clap Flynn on the arm. "Enjoy yourself. I better greet the rest of the guests."

Flynn smiles. "I know how you feel. It's nice to be the guest at one of these things for a change."

Ilsa and I make the rounds, unfortunately, having to have an uneasy conversation with Vladimir. It's like he enjoys making people uncomfortable. He seemed oddly protective over the woman on his arm, whose name he wouldn't even tell us.

When she went to speak, he shot her a look that could kill. I don't want to know what's going on between them.

My mother clinks a spoon against a glass, and I know it's almost time. Her eyes meet mine, and she gives me a small nod.

"Everyone, I have a very important matter to address before we can have dinner," I say

Our guests turn silent, eyes on us. I can feel Ilsa's gaze burning into me. She will be wondering what I'm playing at, and she's about to find out.

I'm scared. I can't deny it. The thought of Ilsa refusing me makes me sick to the stomach. I turn to face her.

She gives me a questioning look. "What are you doing?" she breathes.

I smile at her and then pull the box out of my jacket.

Her eyes widen as I fall onto one knee.

"Ilsa, you are it for me. My soul mate, my savior, my world."

Tears glisten in her eyes.

"I'm so glad I found you. This adventure is only starting, but I want to ask you if the rest of it you will journey as my wife." I flip open the top of the box to reveal my grandmother's engagement ring. It's ruby and diamonds since blood-born Jeremiah children have always been red dragons, it seems fitting. My mother wasn't the original royal, hence why she is emerald green when shifted. "Will you marry me, Ilsa?"

She clutches at her chest, eyes wide. For a moment, I wonder if she's even going to respond.

"Of course, Aiden."

I stand, pulling the ring out of the box.

Ilsa watches as I slip it onto her finger. It fits perfectly. She smiles and launches herself into my arms, kissing me passionately.

Our guests erupt into cheers and applause as we kiss. Finally, she breaks free and turns deep red. It's as if she just remembered where we were. She's adorable.

I can't deny, sometimes I do forget. When she looks at me, it feels like we're the only people left in the room or on this planet. I can't wait to spend the rest of my life feeling like that with her.

EPILOGUE

ILSA

"*How* ow are you feeling, sweetheart?" my mom asks as I stare at myself in the mirror.

I draw in a deep breath. "Nervous as hell."

My mom smiles and squeezes my shoulder. "It's natural to be nervous."

I sigh. "Why couldn't I have fallen in love with a recluse instead of a king?"

She laughs. "You two are soul mates, that's why."

Thousands of people wait in the castle's grounds, ready to watch me and Aiden tie the knot. I rest my hands on my belly, knowing that soon, I'll have to tell Aiden.

We've been so busy with planning this wedding, I haven't found a moment to tell him I'm pregnant. I found out last week.

Someone knocks on the door.

"Come in," my mom calls.

Lucy appears at the door and slips into the room. "You look stunning," she says, dragging her eyes down my dress. "They are ready for you when you are."

I swallow hard and glance back at the mirror. "Will I ever be ready?" I mutter.

Lucy comes to my side and slips an arm around me. "I know how you feel. You don't want to walk out in front of all those people."

I raise a brow.

"I had a royal wedding, too, remember."

I nod, knowing that Lucy has had many similar experiences to me. "Yeah, I know. How did you get the courage to step out there?" I ask.

She smiles. "The moment I saw Flynn, everyone else just seemed to fade into the background. It felt like—"

"You were the only two people in the room," I finish.

"Exactly. You'll be fine."

Her confidence fills me with some. "What would I do without you, Lucy?" I ask, hugging my maid of honor.

She has been a real friend through all of this— something I've never really had until I met Aiden. We've been too paranoid as a family, keeping everyone else out. There's no need for it now. The witches and warlock's population will revive now Aiden's father isn't trying to oppress us. There are rebels, but that's natural with change. In time, I hope all of us can work together to make this world a better place for our children.

"You'd be just fine, although the wedding wouldn't be as much of a success."

I laugh. "That I agree with. You've done such a good job helping to plan everything."

My dad pokes his head through the door. "What's the hold-up. It's time."

Butterflies beat around in my stomach as I nod. "Okay, I can do this. I hope."

"Of course you can. Now, where are Killian and Niamh? See you there." She rushes out of the room, searching for the flower girl and page boy.

My dad steps inside. "Are you ready?"

I glance back at my mom.

She gives me a reassuring nod.

"Ready as I'll ever be."

"I best go and get in place in the procession. You'll be just fine, Ilsa." She squeezes my hand. "I'm so proud of the woman you've become."

I watch after her as she slips out of the room, leaving me with my father.

He steps forward. "You look amazing, Ilsa. Come on. We don't want to keep the king waiting." He holds out his arm for me to take.

I take it, thankful that I've still got my family here for this. If I hadn't come after them, they'd be dead now, and I would have never met Aiden. I push the thought from my mind and focus on what has happened. We saved my parents, and we're together.

I'm sad that I never got to meet his sister, Elaine.

From what Aiden and his mother have told me about her, we would have got on. Her husband is here today. He took it hard, especially since she was his mate.

I can't fathom how he must feel—it would be like someone taking Aiden from me. A lifetime isn't long enough to spend with him.

"How are you feeling, sweetheart?" Dad asks.

I draw in a deep breath. "Nervous as hell. You know how bad I am with crowds, especially with their attention on me." I sigh. "Don't let me make a fool of myself."

"I won't let you do that, but all you have to do is walk down an aisle." He frowns. "I'm not sure what can go wrong."

I shake my head and laugh. "You know how much of a klutz I am. Anything could go wrong."

He chuckles softly. "You'll be fine."

I feel the nerves building as I gaze down toward the lawn where they've set up the aisle and a massive flower arch. We're too far away for me to see Aiden, but I've got no doubt he can see me. His vision is better than I ever could have imagined.

I clutch my dad's arm as he walks me down the steps of the castle. If it weren't for him steadying me, I'm pretty sure I'd be flat on the floor right now.

I can feel my body shaking as we approach the arch, and I see the thousands of bodies seated beyond it. For a moment, I seriously think about turning and running the other way. I'm not cut out for this queen shit.

Then our eyes meet. Aiden's staring right at me before the music even plays—before anyone else knows we've arrived.

He smiles and gives me a nod of encouragement.

It's all it takes to still the nerves firing inside of me. I smile back, feeling my heart swell at the sight of him in a stunning red suit—his family's color.

The music starts to play as my dad pulls me to a stop. My mother is at the front, and she starts the procession, walking slowly to the music.

All eyes are now on the aisle, and shortly they will be on me.

Anastasia follows next, as my bridesmaid. Shortly after is Lucy, my maid of honor, followed close by her children. Killian and Niamh both look adorable dressed in their outfits.

My dad gives me a nod and a gentle tug to get me moving.

I step onto the aisle, glancing around at all the faces. There's not only dragons and witches but many faeries, vampires, and humans in attendance.

I almost stumble on my next step, feeling the heat shooting through my body—too many people watching me. I feel like I'm about to have a breakdown.

I focus forward and meet Aiden's gaze again. Keeping my eyes on his is the only thing that's going to get me down the aisle. Our eyes remain locked, and all the other people here fade away. It's as if we are in our own little world.

Lucy peels off to the left with the two children, leaving nothing between us.

My dad pulls me to a stop in front of the officiant.

"Who gives this man to this woman?"

"I do," my dad says, passing my hand into Aiden's.

The moment we touch, it takes away any nerves. His eyes hold pure adoration as we stare at each other.

I hardly hear the officiant as he runs through the traditional royal ceremony until I need to speak.

"Ilsa Black, do you take Aiden Logan Jeremiah to be your wedded husband?" he asks.

I smile at Aiden. "I do."

He turns his attention to Aiden. "Aiden Logan Jeremiah, do you take Ilsa Black to be your wedded wife?"

He pauses for a moment, and it feels like I'm suffering a cardiac rest while he drags it out. "I do."

The officiant smiles. "Then, by the power vested in me by the royal court, I pronounce you husband and wife." He glances at Aiden. "You may kiss the bride, your highness."

Aiden steps forward and kisses me deeply, setting my veins on fire. At that moment, I do forget about the thousands of people watching, letting my arms wrap slip his neck.

When we break away, I'm a little breathless.

Everyone is cheering and clapping, and that's when it all hits me again. Heat floods through my cheeks, as Aiden starts to lead me through them all.

Did I seriously just survive that without making a fool of myself?

Aiden leans towards me. "What are you looking so surprised for?"

I smile. "That I managed to pull that off without falling over or being a klutz."

"You were perfect, love." He kisses my cheek softly as we head through the arch. "This is the start of the rest of our lives together."

My heart swells in my chest, and I feel my throat close over slightly. The emotion this man makes me feel is indescribable.

AIDEN DANCES WITH NIAMH, letting her stand on his feet. I can't help but smile as I watch him, keeping my hand on my belly. He could be doing that with our daughter before I know it.

I know it's a girl, being a witch, I have powerful foresight.

Anastasia sits by my side. "That man will make a great father," she says.

I nod and glance at her. "Yes, he will."

She tilts her head. "You've got a glow about you, even before this wedding. Is there something I don't know?"

I bite my bottom lip and grab her hand. "Please

don't tell Aiden. I only found out last week, and I haven't found a moment to break it to him yet."

She shakes her head. "Of course, your secret is safe with me." She glances around to makes sure no one can hear. "If I were you, I'd tell him tonight. When I told Rhys I was pregnant, we had the night of our lives." She winks. "Just a little tip, as wolf shifters love getting their mates pregnant. I'm sure it's no different for dragons."

I laugh at that and nod. "Thanks for the tip."

She glances over at the stroller, where her son is fast asleep. "I never expected to be a mother to four children." The other children are playing close by. "I wouldn't change it for the world, though."

I clear my throat. "Four?"

She meets my gaze. "No, surely not?"

I bite my bottom lip and nod. "You are pregnant again, another boy."

She sighs and then smiles. "A little playmate for Lewis. Rhys will be delighted."

Aiden comes back with Niamh, and her father takes over, taking her to dance. She loves dancing.

Anastasia leans toward me. "I'll leave you to it," she whispers, as Aiden approaches.

He sits down next to me, and Anastasia slips away. "Hello, wife."

I smile. "Hello, husband."

He takes my hand in his and kisses the back of it. "We need to leave for our honeymoon shortly."

I look into his bright orange eyes. "Where are we going?"

He smiles. "Not far, but somewhere you will love."

Nerves flutter in my stomach as I consider telling him about the baby. We haven't even talked about children yet. Although, I know he needs an heir being royalty.

"What's on your mind?"

I meet his gaze again. "I've got some news."

He squeezes my hand tightly. "What is it?"

I shake my head. "Not here, let's go somewhere—"

"We'll set off for our honeymoon now then. We'll inform everyone." The concern in his voice makes me guilty. He stands, dragging me with him.

"Aiden, wait, it's not urgent."

He turns around and kisses me urgently. "My need to consummate this marriage is, and you've just given me the perfect excuse to leave."

A shiver runs down my spine at the tone of his voice. "Okay."

He heads up to the stage in the marquee and intercepts the band. "I need to make an announcement."

The woman stops singing, and the musicians stop playing.

Aiden clears his throat before speaking into the microphone, "Thank you, everyone, for attending our wedding. Ilsa and I are going to leave for our honeymoon now. I hope you enjoy the party until the early hours. See you when we return."

Everyone cheers and claps as Aiden scoops me up into his arms and carries me off the stage.

"What are you carrying me for?"

He laughs. "It's a tradition for me to carry you—"

"Over the threshold of our home, not out of the wedding party."

He shrugs. "It's my new tradition, then."

I can't help but laugh as he carries me out into the grounds. "I have to shift to take us where we are going."

"You better undress then. You can't ruin that beautiful suit."

He nods. "I agree." He holds my gaze as he gets out of his clothes, revealing his perfect, sculpted body. I'll never tire of seeing him naked. "Grab the clothes, love, while I shift."

I rush over and grab his clothes, folding them.

Aiden roars behind me as he shifts into his magnificent dragon form. He sets his right-wing down on the floor and leans over to help me climb on in this dress, which isn't easy.

As I get on his back, I realize this dress won't allow me to straddle his neck. It looks like I'm going side-saddle on a fucking dragon's back.

I clutch onto his scales as best I can as he launches into the air, flapping his vast wings. He rises into the night sky over the mountain before soaring downward toward the lake's sparkling surface.

I get a feeling I know where we are heading. The bay we went to the first time we met. He swerves toward it and unleashes his fire across the glistening surface, making the water bubble.

My heart skips a beat as I see the beach lit with candles all over it. A small cabin sits close to the water. Aiden has pulled out all the stops for this.

He lands on the beach, and I slide off his back onto the sand. I take my white, lace pumps off as they are too beautiful to wear on the sand.

I watch as Aiden turns back to his beautiful human form. It never gets boring, watching him shift.

"What do you think?" he asks.

I look around, smiling. "Perfect. I can't believe you got a cabin built here."

He smiles. "I built it by hand, like the one in the forest. Didn't you wonder where I'd been off to recently?"

"Yes, but I just assumed you were busy with important king duties or getting ready for the wedding." I raise a brow. "Not building a cabin."

He laughs. "I did get a hand from Flynn to be fair, without his magic, I'm not sure I would have got it done in time."

I feel the electric tension pulse between us as we stare into each other's eyes. We're alone on our wedding night, which means only one thing.

Aiden comes rushing for me, crashing into me and kissing me hard and deep.

I push him away. "Aiden, wait. I've got to tell you my news."

"Oh shit, yeah, sorry, you look so beautiful, I forgot."

I laugh and nod toward a beach sofa to our left. "Shall we sit?"

He grabs my hand and leads me over to it. "What is it, Ilsa?"

I set my hand on my belly and meet his gaze. "I found out last week. I'm pregnant."

His eyes widen, and then a huge smile creeps onto his lips. "Are you serious?"

I nod. "Yeah, I know we haven't talked—"

He kisses me suddenly, silencing me. "This is amazing." He cups my chin in his hands. "Do you know the sex?"

I nod. "Does it matter to you?"

He shakes his head. "No, I'll be happy with either"

"It's a girl."

He lifts me for the sofa and spins me around, shocking me with his strength. "This is the happiest day of my life. It already is marrying you, but finding out we are going to be welcoming our first child soon makes it that much better."

"I love you, Aiden."

He smiles and kisses me. "I love you too, Ilsa. Always." He pulls me in for a hard, passionate kiss. My desire increases as I feel his hard body against mine. "We need to get you out of this dress before I make a mess of it." He glances down at his hard, leaking cock dripping between us.

I moan, seeing him so ready for me.

"Yes," I breathe, turning around for him to unzip it.

He makes quick work of getting me out of it, groaning when he sees my white lace underwear and suspenders to match. "Fuck, you look perfect."

I bite my bottom lip as he comes at me, his eyes wild with need. I moan as his hands are all over me, his hard muscles pressing against my soft skin, his cock resting against my tummy. He makes quick work of getting me out of my expensive lingerie, leaving it on the sofa. "Fuck me, Aiden, please. No teasing, make love to me."

His eyes glint with mischief, but he nods. "Okay, but only because it's our wedding night." He spanks my ass softly before lifting me off the ground. "I've got plenty of time to tease you afterward."

Aiden carries me into the water before letting me down. "Stunning," he breathes as he kisses my neck, trailing down to my shoulders.

I gasp as he bites my collarbone. "Aiden, I need you inside of me now."

He raises a brow. "No foreplay at all?"

I shake my head and grab his hand, letting him feel how ready I am for him.

He growls and then lifts me off the floor again, carrying me deeper into the water where he can stand.

I moan as he lowers me onto his huge cock.

He's so big, but I'm so wet he slides inside of me with no problem. "Fuck, you are so perfect." He bites my bottom lip hard, making me moan.

It's crazy how good it is when he mixes pain and

pleasure. The way it makes the pleasure that much more intense. I stare into his eyes as he moves me up and down his cock, desperation increasing between us by the second.

The stars and moon twinkling above shine on his tan skin, making him look more beautiful than I've ever seen.

"Aiden," I breathe his name, as his hands wander to my buttocks.

He lifts me up and down his shaft slowly but forcefully, making me feel every single inch as he slides in and out. We maintain eye contact the whole time. The desire and adoration in his eyes flood me with pure bliss.

"Ilsa," he groans my name against my lips. "I love you."

The pressure inside of me builds, sending me to a height beyond anything I've felt before. "I love you, too." Tears of joy prickle at my eyes.

He kisses me softly as we continue to move together as one, our souls merging. It feels magical. It gets more intense, the longer we're together. It's only been a couple of months since we met, but I can't see this desire ever letting up.

Aiden grunts as he holds off, driving me toward my climax with every thrust.

My head falls back as he picks up the tempo, increasing his thrusts and the speed at which he drives me up and down. He kisses my throat and mutters against my skin, "Come for me, love. I want you to come on your husband's cock."

I melt at the sound of his rough, hard voice. The demand underlying. He sucks on my nipples, and that's all it takes. "Fuck, Aiden," I cry out, feeling my muscles clamp down around him.

He growls as he explodes at the same time, our climaxes timed perfectly. We're both breathless and hot, as we cling onto each other in the warm, still water.

Slowly, I regain composure, keeping my arms wrapped around his neck. "That was..."

"Perfect," he finishes.

I smile. "Yeah."

He kisses me for a long time, slowly and softly. Our love only seems to grow every moment we spend together—I didn't think it was possible to love someone the way I love him.

"Come on, love. Let's go inside." He kisses me softly before lifting me again in his arms.

I don't protest about being carried even though I could walk. I enjoy the moment instead, feeling Aiden's strong, protective arms around me. He walks toward the cabin and pushes the door open with his foot.

Aiden carries me over the threshold, which is as beautiful inside—a perfect new hideout to enjoy together. I can't wait to welcome the new addition to our family—and share all of this love with her. Life is infinitely better with Aiden, and I can't wait to navigate the rest of it with him by my side.

THE END

Thank you for reading Her Dragon King, the third book in The Royally Mated series. I hope you enjoyed following Aiden & Ilsa's story. The next book follows Vladimir & Rosie's story and will be available through Kindle Unlimited or to pre-order on Amazon.

Her Vampire King: A Dark Vampire Romance

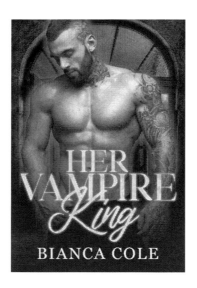

They told me not to enter London and now I know why.

The scent of blood is overwhelming. Only the most powerful vampires could stand a chance of resisting. My steel willpower is being tested, but no one is as strong as me.

Until I scent her. A blood that calls to me. A blood that drives me insane. A blood I can't resist.

I stalk her through the streets, tracking her. When I get my hands on her, the need is too difficult to resist. She's the most beautiful woman I've ever seen. Vampires don't mate, but this connection feels deep and sacred.

My people have wanted me to take a wife for decades. It looks like I've just found her. They won't like it, but I don't care. I'm claiming this tasty, stunning human as my own.

They will want to stop me, I'd like to see them try. No one can defeat me. I'll protect her, if it's the last thing I do.

Wynton Series

Filthy Boss: A Forbidden Office Romance

Filthy Professor: A First Time Professor And Student Romance

Filthy Lawyer: A Forbidden Hate to Love Romance

Romano Mafia Brother's Series

Her Mafia Daddy: A Dark Daddy Romance

Her Mafia Boss: A Dark Romance

Her Mafia King: A Dark Romance

Bratva Brotherhood Series

Bought by the Bratva: A Dark Mafia Romance

Captured by the Bratva: A Dark Mafia Romance

Claimed by the Bratva: A Dark Mafia Romance

Bound by the Bratva: A Dark Mafia Romance

Royally Mated Series

Her Faerie King: A Royal Wolf Shifter Paranormal Romance

Her Alpha King: A Dragon Shifter Paranormal Romance

Her Vampire King: A Dark Vampire Romance

ABOUT THE AUTHOR

Bianca Cole loves to write stories about over the top alpha bad boys who have heart beneath it all, fiery heroines, and happily-ever-after endings with heart. Her stories have twists and turns that will keep you flipping the pages, and just enough heat to set your kindle on fire.

If you enjoyed this book please follow her on Amazon or Facebook for alerts when more books are released - Click here for her Amazon Author Page.

Printed in Great Britain
by Amazon